BEAUTIFUL CITY OF THE DEAD

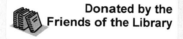

All rights reserved. Published in the United States by Graphia, an imprint of
Houghton Mifflin Company, Boston, Massachusetts. Originally published in
hardcover in the United States by Houghton Mifflin Company, Boston, in 2006.

Graphia and the Graphia logo are registered trademarks
of Houghton Mifflin Company.

For information about permission to reproduce selections
from this book, write to Permissions, Houghton Mifflin Company,
215 Park Avenue South, New York, New York 10003.

www.houghtonmifflinbooks.com

The text of this book is set in ApolloMT.
Illustrations by Sammy Yuen Jr.

Library of Congress Cataloging-in-Publication Data.
Watts, Leander.
Beautiful city of the dead / by Leander Watts.
p. cm.
Summary: After joining a heavy metal band, high school student
Zee learns that she is a god of water and is called upon to fight
sinister forces that want her powers for their own.
ISBN-13: 978-0-618-59443-6 (hardcover)
ISBN-13: 978-0-618-59499-x (paperback)
[1. Supernatural—Fiction. 2. Heavy metal (Music)—Fiction.
3. Bands (Music)—Fiction. 4. High schools—Fiction.
5. Schools—Fiction.] I. Title.
PZ7.W339Bea 2006
[Fic]—dc22
2005020993

Manufactured in the United States of America.
HAD 10 9 8 7 6 5 4 3 2 1

fire   *earth*   *wind*   *water*

BEAUTIFUL CITY
OF THE DEAD

A NOVEL BY
LEANDER WATTS

An imprint of the Houghton Mifflin Company
Boston

fire   *earth*   *wind*   *water*

Part One

One

IT STARTS WITH FIRE.

Scrape a match on the rough sandpaper side of the box. Snap back the little tongue on a Bic. Hold a lens in strong sunlight and wait for the hot beam to set a scrap of paper ablaze.

A burning whisper, a tongue of fire, a screaming mouth of flames.

Yeah, that's where it starts.

I'm not a pyro. That's what people think when I talk about fire. They figure I'm some messed up pyro-girl who gets off on burning burning burning. First it's matches, then the candles, then a torch made of gas-soaked rags.

Truth be told, I'm actually afraid of fire. I mean, I've always been drawn to it. I can't hardly keep my eyes away. There's definitely something there that pulls me closer. But at the same time, it makes me feel weak. And afraid.

A roaring red wind. A swirling current of flames.

Heat, raw heat. And the buzz and the crackle and the moan of pure fire.

I know about pyros. Those kind of people are sick, and they're crazy. And it's not like that for me. Not at all.

But still, it starts with fire.

Two

SO IT WAS THE FIRST DAY at a new school and I didn't know anyone. There's thousands of kids all rushing and pushing and yelling and I had a fever of 102°. I should have been in bed I guess. But my dad said I needed to be in school. I was up all night going from sweats to chills, watching the little orange dial of my clock. 3, 4, 5, 6. And the fever got worse just about when the sun came up.

Burning red, cold September light. I rolled out of my sweat-drenched bed and an hour later I was standing in line for something, it doesn't matter what now. Just a line. A hundred kids, shoving and grumbling.

And me, burning up. The Amazing Fever Girl. Weak, wet, and woozy.

"You into Brain Hammer, too?" a kid asked me. I'd drawn band logos inside one of my notebooks. Kind of secret. The cover was perfectly plain. Not a mark on it. But inside, in bold, hard lettering: Brain Hammer, the Fabulous Rectotem, Breather Hole, Little Black Pills.

No one had ever seen inside before. No one had ever bothered to look, when I was writing in it.

"Yeah," I said. It felt weird to have him peeking at my gallery of band names. But I didn't close the notebook. "Saw them last year at Waterstreet. Put on a good show."

He was skinny, with long black hair and eyes like a night creature's. Big and and shiny and red. Some people have beautiful blue or green eyes, like gemstones. But this kid's eyes were deep red, almost purple. Mine are the exact opposite, kind of washed-out watery brown. "Real good show," he said. "My ears were ringing for a week."

The fever was making everything blurry. The kid kind of shimmered there in front of me, like when you see something through waves of heat. "My name's Relly," he said, almost in a whisper. I had him repeat it.

"Relly?"

"That's right," he said. He didn't exactly smile. In fact, I never saw him smile. But he stayed there with me. And he kept talking.

"I'm Zee."

"What?"

I spelled my name for him. "It was my dad's idea. I think he got it from an old mystery novel. Least, that's what he says."

So we both were into Brain Hammer. And we both were members of the Weird Name Club. If you're a John or a Sarah or a David or an Emily, you just don't know what it's like to have people look at you funny every time you say who you are. "How do you spell that? Does that mean something? That's your full name?"

I was feeling so weak I had to lean against the wall or I'd end up in a heap. "You in Bio this period?" I asked.

"Yeah." He edged in closer and looked at me like he was trying to see through a foggy window. "You look awful," he said.

"Thanks."

"No, I mean you look kind of sick."

"Just the flu. I should be home in bed."

He said some more, but it was all a blur. Names of people I didn't know, words I didn't understand, bands I'd never heard of.

I made it to the end of the day in my fever fog. I didn't remember anything but Relly. Those big eyes staring into me, like he saw something nobody else could see.

Three

TURNS OUT THAT I WAS together with Relly in two classes. Bio and art.

I missed the second day of school. But then the fever broke and my dad said I'd have to go back.

In art, the teacher said he wanted everybody to do a project about something they didn't understand. It could be technical, like perspective or shading. Or it could be a subject. There was the usual stuff: racism and abortion and God and eating meat. "I don't understand," one whiny-voiced girl said, "cruelty to our fellow creatures."

I went a little more specific. I brought in an old *Look* magazine I'd found at my grandparents'. It was from the Vietnam War days, all warped and wrinkly and stinking of their moldy basement. The thing I didn't understand was a picture of three Buddhist monks sitting cross-legged on the sidewalk, wrapped up in fire. Their faces shone through the billowing flame, like skulls seen through wispy veils. The real thing from the olden days. Full page, full color.

The teacher was clearly freaked out. But he tried to be cool and ask me what I didn't understand.

"They did it to themselves," I said. "It was a protest against the war. Get it? But why? How would anyone do it?" There were a couple of gas cans to one side, surrounded by a pool of liquid fire.

He made some lame suggestions about "the triumph of the human spirit." And he said I could make a collage, like I was a fourth grader. And went on to talk with Heather Potts about her collection of Kalico Kitten pictures.

Relly came over and looked at my burning monks. "Crot Almighty," he said. He made up words like *crot* and *draghole* and *poxy* and used them even if you didn't understand. "Where'd you get this?"

"Old magazine."

"And you want to understand it?"

"That is so messed up," a guy named Nick Byers said, looking over Relly's shoulder. "Why would you bring that to school?" I guess he thought girls shouldn't be into such flat-out freakout stuff. Makeup, soccer, TV, baby-sitting. Those were OK for girls. But burning monks, Brain Hammer, playing the bass. Those were supposed to be just for guys. And weird guys at that.

Relly looked close at the picture. "They look almost happy," he whispered.

"Yeah. Not quite. But almost. Maybe it's better than happiness," I said.

That should have been enough to scare him off. But it didn't. He kept asking me about the picture. And he was really listening to my answers.

Four

SO THAT'S HOW WE MET. And that's why he started telling me all about his band.

"You know how if you turn the volume all the way up till your ears almost bleed, how when it's so loud there's a quiet place inside the noise? Loud enough to shake your teeth loose but in there somewhere is a ghost voice, like silence singing."

Relly kept going, testing me. If I just walked away, shaking my head, then he'd know I was like all the rest. But I stayed there and listened, and maybe even tried to understand. "That's the sound I want to get. So loud it almost crushes your skull flat and inside the noise is a ghost, a candle flame burning inside a fiery furnace." He said he was inventing a whole new kind of music, something he called Ghost Metal. Screaming guitars, crusher bass, drums like a ten-car pileup. But inside the noise, a ghost voice, something almost silent but still you can hear it.

"You want to know something?" We were eating

lunch. Or I guess by then we were poking at the wreckage of lunch. "They call me Freak Boy and they're right."

His voice was way low, like he was telling me some evil secret. "I am the Freak Boy. And that's totally OK. Freak Boy conquers the universe. Freak Boy burns like a meteor whipping through the atmosphere. Freak Boy and his band defeats the power of Uberwanks. Freak Boy gets a thousand girls and makes them scream." He was all cranked up, still whispering, but his eyes were shining and the words came out fast.

"So I don't care what they call me. Freak Boy is just fine. It means that they see me for what I am. They're afraid of what I'll do. They know that some day I'll be out of this poxhole and killing the crowd every night ten thousand at a time with my guitar."

I guess I should have been afraid of him. And maybe I was. Afraid and still I wanted to be near him. Afraid and still I wanted to hear him go on about Ghost Metal and the King Cruncher Riff, and how he'd be on top some day, all the way on the top.

Five

ABOUT A WEEK INTO the new school year, I saw a wrecked car by the side of the road. My bus had to slow down to get around the police. And everybody was gawking out the windows. The car was burning, thick greasy smoke churning up from the motor. I guess the people were out and safe. So the police just stood there watching the car burn.

I may be weird in some ways. But like everyone else, I had to look. And I kept looking as long as I could, craning my neck to get a last glimpse of the black cloud and the crimson flames.

So what? You don't see a burning car every day. But it wasn't like a flying saucer had landed at the mall or Elvis came back from the dead on Sesame Street. So why should it make any difference?

Only because of what I was feeling when I saw it. I've read a lot about pyros and how they get off on fires. Most of the times it's loser guys who've got something twisted and rotten inside themselves. And fire is supposed to be an outlet for this messed-up part of them. I've read a ton about it. Psycho stuff, medical and police stuff. I even found a little booklet they gave out to junior high kids in the olden days. "Arson Is No Joke."

What you've got to understand is that I never, ever played with matches. I didn't even try smoking when the other girls were. I didn't start all four burners on the stove and stand there staring into the blue hissing flames. I didn't even like campfires and toasting marshmallows.

So when I talk about fire, it's not the standard pyro stuff.

In fact, sometimes I think I'm drawn to fire because it's the opposite of who and what I really am. Do I feel the pull, I used to wonder, because it's the thing I don't have? The thing I need to make me complete? I heard a guy on TV say that when people really fall in love it's two opposites fitting perfectly together, like the north and south ends of a magnet. They're totally different, but they need each other. Like night and day. Like burning sun and drenching rain to make green things grow.

So maybe that's why the fiery car really got to me. I wanted to know what the smoke smelled like and what the tongues of flame felt like, licking out of the wreck.

I told Relly about it the next day. "All the seats and plastic and dashboard burning: that's the dangerous part. The smoke is poison. Not the fire itself. That actually makes things pure. You know, like heating up a needle when you got to get a sliver out of your finger."

He nodded. "Totally," he said. "Or at the dentist's office, you know, they put the tools in the machine to sterilize them. Boiling water to kill all the germs."

"To make it pure, right?"

"Yeah. Fire and water. You need them both. Together."

Six

"WE THREW OUT OUR BASS PLAYER," he told me the next day. "He cared more about his hair than the music. I should've known. He was such a poser with those black leather pants. Butt never liked him." Butt was the drummer. "Jerod did. That should've been a sign too. What does a singer know about bass?"

So there it was: my big chance. I didn't believe in fate. I didn't think that the planets lined up and shaped our lives. Or secret forces were working. I'm not sure I even believed in genes and DNA. People just are. Things just happen.

"So you're looking for somebody? I mean for the band?" I asked.

"Yeah, I guess. But it's such a pain trying out new guys. They come in trying to impress you with their awesome chops." He kind of sneered, saying that. "I mean, you got to be able to play. But just wiggling your fingers fast is nothing. It's worse than nothing. Pure crot."

"It's got to be a guy?"

"What do you mean?"

"Maybe I should try out for the band." There, I said it. Let him laugh, or snicker. But I said it.

"What are you talking about?"

"I play bass. I've been in some bands." This second bit was sort of a lie.

"You never told me that." We were hanging around by his locker. He closed it, real quiet. He looked at me in a different way than before. And I liked it.

"I never told you a lot of things."

"You're serious? You can really play?"

I was serious. And yeah, I could play.

But he didn't give me the OK yet. "I'll have to talk to Butt and Jerod. There was this other guy we were going to check out."

"Sure. I understand."

Seven

I plugged in that night and let it rip. I figured I could make with the rolling thundergod sound for about fifteen minutes before the neighbors called the police. It felt good to wrap my hands around the neck of my Ibanez. It felt good to stand in front of the amp and have the bass throb deep inside me.

Other than me and the Ibanez, the house was empty. Most nights that was how it went. My dad worked as a cook at the Chimes Diner and usually was gone before suppertime. So I had the house to myself.

I dug through my records. Led Zeppelin, Black Sabbath, Judas Priest: the ancient kings of metal, all on vinyl from the olden days.

I cranked my tunes pretty loud when my dad wasn't home. I played along, real heavy and hard. And I synched up my heartbeat with the steel throb. The bass and my pulse together as one.

Eight

I kept asking myself, *What kind of a name is Relly?* I wrote it out a couple of times in my special notebook, just to look at it. Big letters. Small. Fancy. Plain. I even did one version like it was made out of chrome, raised letters all shiny. But anyway I wrote it, the name didn't make any sense.

Lots of kids I know had stupid Deadhead names like Casey Jones and Panama and Garcia. Then there was the J squad: Jeremy and Jessica, Jason and Jennifer. Some were from the flower-power days: Moonwise, or Windstar. I swear I knew a kid in seventh grade named Breathe.

So the next day I asked, "What does 'Relly' mean?"

"What difference does it make?" he said.

"I don't know. I just figured I should—"

"Well, where does your name come from?"

"I told you. My dad got it from some murder mystery. You know, square-jawed guys with guns, beautiful ladies in slinky silk dresses. All he does when he's not working is read old paperbacks."

Relly gave me that dead-serious look again, like he was a sniper and aiming down the sights of his gun. "You really want to know?"

"Yeah. I never met anyone before who——"

"It came to my mom in a dream." He waited for me to laugh. I didn't. He kept going. "The night before I was born, she had this dream. The name came out of nowhere. Later, she looked it up in a hundred books, old ones, new ones, and the name can't be found."

"So you think it means something?"

"It's got to, right? Every name means something."

"I guess so."

We were hanging around in the hall, waiting for the buses. Most everyone was gone home by then. "I asked Butt and Jerod about you trying out for the band," he said. "They're not thrilled about it. Still, they said it was OK. You got to understand: Butt's like a little kid. I mean he's the best drummer I've ever played with. Only he's kind of immature. I mean, his jokes are pretty scabby. You'll have to get used to that. And Jerod said he'd been in a band with a girl once before and he hated it."

"If you don't think it's a good idea, we'll just forget it."

"That's not what I'm saying."

"All right. Then when do I come over?" I asked.

"Tomorrow night. You don't have to haul your amp. I've got one you can use."

Nine

HE TOLD ME HE LIVED on Slime Street. It was really called South Lime, but the sign on the corner was pretty beat. The period was missing after the *S*. So Relly ran the letters together and made *Slime*.

His block wasn't exactly a slum. But it sure wasn't the best part of town. Once the sun was down on Slime Street, there wasn't anyone around except Relly and his mom and a few stray cats.

There weren't any real neighbors. Just abandoned warehouses and old boarded-up stores. Hardly any cars, nobody walking. All the buildings kind of leaned together like sick creaky old men. Most of the windows were dead black. That first night I went, a tongue of cold air came licking down from the north and got caught on Slime Street. It turned and turned, and made a little whirlwind, sucking up paper cups and dead leaves and bits of plastic.

His house was three stories tall. And real narrow. So,

between two empty lots, it looked like a tower.

I stood at the front door for a while, thinking I should just turn around and go home. They wouldn't want me. We'd go through a couple of tunes and they'd give me that fake little smile that means "Thanks, but no thanks."

It was actually a double door, with an arched top, like the entrance to an old church. The paint looked about a hundred years old, peeling off in long curls. No doorbell. He'd told me that already. "There's some rocks on the front step. Just use one of those to bang on the door. My mom will hear it."

And she did. The door came open. "You're the girl," she said. No "hello," or "come on in." She just stood there looking me over. "You're the girl," she said again.

That wasn't obvious? "Yeah. Relly said I should—"

She opened the door wider and I figured that meant I should go in.

My bass case kind of banged against the door. I was trying to pass through without getting too close to Relly's mom. "Sorry, sorry," I said. But she wasn't the type to care about a few digs in the woodwork.

She was no suburban mom. Not by a long shot.

Like Relly, she was tall and thin. And she had the same long black hair. From the way he'd talked about her, I thought she'd be an old stoner metalhead. She actually remembered going to see Orion Hedd. "Totally changed my life." He repeated this to me. And it sounded like he'd heard her say it about a hundred times. "I'll tell you that. Nothing was ever better. It was like a shimmering magic wind came blowing through. Right down from the stars, a cold wind from the seventh heaven."

But with me, she didn't get into the '70s trippy weirdness. At least not that first night.

She pointed to the stairs. "You'd better leave your coat on. It gets cold up there." And that was that.

Ten

SO I CLIMBED THE three flights of steps to the attic. The stairs didn't creak. They whispered. Or that's what it seemed like as I went up. Faint voices from far away.

At the first-floor landing, I heard the steady thump of Butt's kick drum. At the second, a low growling riff reached my ears. By the third floor, the whisper of the stairs was drowned out by drums and guitar and someone's maniac yells.

I got to the attic and pushed open the door. A wave of sound broke and poured around me. They were good. Already I could tell.

"Hey, all right!" Relly said. "You came."

"I said I would."

He pointed to Butt, behind his drum set. "There he is. Don't smell so good and can't hardly talk. But he can drub those drums better than the best." Relly had a different way of speaking now. A little louder. Kind of brash and bragging. This was his turf, unlike school. These were his friends, his allies, his band mates. He could be more himself here than in a school filled with two thousand strangers. "And this is Mr. Jerod Powers, the Golden Boy."

Jerod was so good-looking I almost had to turn away. I mean it was too much, all that wild blond hair and piercing blue eyes and pouty lips. I guess every band needs a pretty boy. Didn't matter if he could sing. But as it turned out, he was pretty good.

"So what do you think?"

I didn't answer at first. What did he want me to say? "Yeah, Butt's a shaved gorilla and Jerod should be in the movies?"

Then I understood. He meant the attic, and what they'd done to make it a practice space. "It's great, it's great," I said. And I wasn't just talking. It truly was an amazing place.

The ceiling went way up, with dozens of weird angles like a cathedral. It was all raw boards. And the ooze of hundred-year-old sap hung down in hard amber drops.

They'd pushed mountains of abandoned junk to the edges of the attic to make room for the band. There was a wardrobe full of old clothes, wooden crates and cardboard boxes, stacks of books, toys, rusty tools. I saw a floor lamp in the wreckage. The shaft looked like bone and the shade like dried animal skin. An old army helmet hung on the wall, along with a velvet painting of a snarling black panther, and a wedding dress in a tattered plastic bag.

The other band I'd played in, and that was only for a few weeks, had practiced in a cellar. Relly's attic was full of junk, too. But it felt just the opposite of some wet, smelly basement. With no close neighbors, they didn't have to insulate for the noise at Relly's. No mattresses on the walls. No foam on the windows or layers of Curbside Special carpet nailed to soak up the sound.

What I liked best was the space over our heads. It seemed to go up and up forever.

Eleven

"YOU CAN PLUG IN OVER HERE," Relly said, pointing to a bass amp all covered with stickers and spray paint.

So I unpacked the Ibanez and uncoiled my cord and got ready.

Jerod said, "It's just a tryout, OK? We're thinking about other guys too. We've got to find exactly the right one. So don't get your hopes up."

And Butt kept looking at me, staring, actually. I guess he was wondering if I had what it took. The bass player and the drummer have to be locked in like two gears in a machine. They've got to mesh and turn together perfectly. He looked at my hands, which aren't huge. And he looked at my bass, which wasn't huge or flashy either. I'd saved for two years to buy the Ibanez. Flipping burgers, "Do you want fries with that?" never getting the smell of grease out of my hair, saying "Have a nice day" to mean, huffy customers. Two years of fast-food stink so I could buy the bass. Butt looked me over and he didn't say a word.

"So what do you know?" Relly asked.

"You guys do any Zeppelin?"

Butt nodded. Relly whanged his Strat, making a big grinding chord. Jerod grabbed the mike with both hands.

"How 'bout 'Black Dog?' " I asked.

A little pause. A little gap of silence, like they were taking in a deep breath, all three of them at once. I thought maybe I'd said the wrong thing, that I'd shown myself to be a feeb and a loser.

But no, it was exactly the right choice. Did they know "Black Dog?" Oh yeah. Could they play it? Oh yes indeed.

Maybe it was all strutting showoff. Or it could have been they wanted to blow away the girl wannabe bass player. Or maybe it was meant to be. Because afterward Relly told me they'd never played like that. Butt nodded, grinning and working his kick drum pedal. And even Jerod had to admit they'd never sounded better.

We ripped into the first tune like we'd been playing together for years. Butt was heavy as ten sledgehammers. Me and Relly doubled the snakey riff, note-for-note perfect. And Jerod was on top, doing his best sexy tomcat yowls.

And the whole band seemed to lift right off the ground. I mean it: like suddenly we went from being lowly humans to brilliant angels. It was an amazing feeling, a scary, gasping buzz. My fingers moved and the logical part of my brain kind of shut down. Pure sound came roaring out. Loud and wild and relentless. And we rose, all four of us, rose up free as flames, no longer trapped, pouring ourselves up and out.

Twelve

UNTIL THAT NIGHT, Relly wouldn't tell me the name. This seemed kind of stupid. How was he going to get famous if he wouldn't reveal the name of his band?

"Not till everything is in place," he'd said. "When we're ready, then we conquer the universe."

He wiped the neck of his Strat and looked at the other two guys. "Well?" he said.

"She's in," Butt said. He did a drumroll and then whacked a crash cymbal. "I say she's in."

Jerod shrugged. "Sure. Whatever."

Relly nodded. "Welcome to Scorpio Bone."

"That's the name of the band?" I asked.

"Scorpio Bone," he said again, louder.

Then he played a dark, crawling riff. Butt joined him, just tom-toms and kick drum, a deep throb. Finally Jerod wailed on top of the noise, "Scorpio Bone!" like this was the theme music to some monster metal movie.

"You're in," Relly said when they'd finished. "Welcome."

We played another hour or two. It was mostly covers. A lot of Black Sabbath and Judas Priest, and one more Led Zeppelin tune, a weird, looming version of "The Ocean."

Then Relly taught me the bass line for one of his originals, "The Three-Prong Crown." It didn't come easy. But it came right. I mean I had to work at it. Still, the line fit my hands and the chords fit the words. And the sound fit my brain.

Thirteen

"BUT SCORPIONS DON'T HAVE BONES," I said the next day at lunch. "They have a shell, right? Like armor. They're arachnids. They don't have any bones."

Up till then I thought Relly was just plain weird. But I didn't know how weird till he started explaining the name. "Don't you see?" he said, whispering like it was some earthshattering secret. "That's what makes the name so cool. It's something that doesn't exist but it's real. Like if scorpions had bones, what would they be? They'd be us."

Butt took two pieces of baloney off his sandwich and ripped holes in the middle. Then he slapped them on his face like a mask and started singing the old *Batman* theme music.

"I don't get it. How can something be real and not real at the—"

"That's the whole point."

We were in the cafeteria, me and Butt and Relly, at a table off in the corner. "Did you believe in Santa Claus when you were little?" He didn't let me answer. "You sure did. And it was cool, right? Some fat magic maniac comes out of the sky with presents and a sleigh and zero-gravity reindeer. Christmas Eve was the best, right? But it's not real. Not like school and pizza and scumpack teachers yelling is real. So our name is ten times more cool. Like in some other world scorpions do have bones."

In some other world? "What are you talking about?"

"Nothing is what it seems to be," Relly leaned close and whispered. "You know, like the whole world is wearing camouflage. Everything and everyone is hiding." Butt wasn't paying much attention. He could only take so much of this weirdness. "They're all like puppets. Only, they don't want you to see their strings. Every person in the world. They all tell lies. They all wear a mask."

Butt nodded, then pulled off his baloney disguise and grinned. Relly pointed over to a table where some of the popular kids were sitting. Good-looking football players, girls with beautiful hair and clear skin and perfect figures. "In a couple years," Relly told me. "They'll all be pumping gas or working as a greeter at K-Mart. 'Hello, have a wonderful day!'" He sneered the words. "And you know where I'll be?"

"No," I said, edging a little closer.

"I don't know, either. But wherever it is, I'll be big. I can tell you that. I will be *immense*." He said that word like a challenge, like he dared anyone to disagree. "I will be so big, all those jocks and jockesses won't even be able to see me. Like ants can't see a person, just a huge shadow looming over before you squash them flat. I will be so big that these losers who think they're such winners won't even recognize me."

One minute I thought he was pathetic. And the next he seemed awesome. Then he was both at the same time. A whispering scrawny kid with a fiery look in his eye.

"Now that we're together, the four of us, it's gonna start. The big time. The biggest thing you ever saw." He kept watching me as he talked, waiting for me to laugh or say this was all stupid. But I didn't.

"It's the Ghost Metal thing," he said. "When we really get cranking, the four of us, we can cross over to the other side, the other world."

He needed Scorpio Bone with him. That's what he said, sitting there watching the clock in the cafeteria. Going over to "the other world" was too dangerous just by himself. "Four sides of the square to make it safe. Seeing in all four directions.

It takes four and no more.
It takes four to win the war."

Were these lyrics from some song he'd written?

I didn't find out that day. The bell rang and we pushed back from the table. Relly went to math and I had English.

Fourteen

BEING AROUND RELLY made me feel very strange. Like when I watched a magician, I knew it was all fake and still I wanted to believe. Card tricks, pulling coins out of midair, sawing a lady in half. It's all bogus, of course. Still, part of me wanted to believe there was such a thing as magic.

Sitting in the cafeteria with Relly, or hanging around his attic after practice, I felt the same way. He talked about the magic four thing, how we had to be "four and no more." Like North, South, East, and West. Or the four Gospels in the Bible. Or the Sex Pistols, who my dad grew up listening to. Or the Four Winds, or the Four Seasons, or the Four Stooges, if you counted Shemp.

"It's always four guys," Relly said. "Every real band is four: bass, guitar, singer, and drums. That's all you need. Orion Hedd and Metallica and Sabbath and the Who. Superheroes, too: the Fantastic Four and those guys in the

Tales of Asgard comics. The Ninja Turtles and the Four Horsemen at the end of the world. War. Conquest. Famine. Death."

It was like those crazy old men in the library downtown who smell bad and babble to themselves for hours. Aliens, secret mind control, werewolves, messages from heaven. It was all a bubbling stew of weirdness.

Yeah, Relly read a lot of comics and watched way too many videos about wizards and warlocks. Yeah, his mom sure didn't discourage him from thinking that way. Yeah, he'd stay up sometimes three days straight with no sleep, which makes your brain do some very strange things.

But still, I never thought his talk of the fourfold gods was a put-on or a figment of his fevered brain. He really believed it. And the more time I spent with him, the more I did, too.

Fifteen

SO I FELT STRANGE when I was around him. But I felt even stranger when I was alone.

Our house is pretty empty at night with my dad gone to work. Sometimes I watched TV, of course, or put on some music.

After Relly said I was in the band, I started practicing more. He gave me some tunes to listen to. He gave me some charts to work from and explained what the symbols meant. Minor and major chords, repeats and intros, that kind of thing. He even said I could bring in songs for the band, if I wanted to write some.

And this was great. It really was, to be part of the band.

Still, sometimes when I'd sit home by myself, a feeling came over me that really scared me. The nights were getting colder and I'd turn on the electric heater in my room. Behind the metal grate there were coils. And they'd glow orange-hot, like a burning snake all wound in on itself.

I'd sit there and look at those glowing coils and I'd wonder what it would feel like to touch them. I know this sounds crazy. It would hurt, and hurt bad. What more did I need to know? Why would anybody want to touch something hot enough to sear the flesh?

I know some girls cut themselves on purpose. And some guys get into fights just to feel the pain of getting hit. That's not what I'm talking about here. Not at all. I know what pain feels like and I don't like it. Not one bit.

One night, the fever came back and my nose ran like a broken faucet. It wasn't the ick and the sweat that bugged me, though. Or the thought that I'd never shake this flu. It was the feeling that I couldn't look away from the orange-hot coils.

There was power in that glow. And I don't mean electric power. Power to burn, to heat, to cook, to hurt. And feverish power to bring something out of me that I'd never seen before.

When my mind would go down that way, it really scared me. That night I thought of calling my dad at work. But he'd be mad. I could go down to the Chimes and just sit in a booth for a while. He'd be in the back, and once in a while I might see him go by the pass-through window. Still, he'd be busy and I'd be out there all by myself.

I picked up my Ibanez and played for a while, pretty

loud, pretty cranked-up. But without the rest of the band, it just didn't do the job.

There was TV. There were books. There were dishes to wash and homework to do.

But no matter what I did, my brain kept dragging me back to those orange, snaky coils, burning hot.

So finally I called Relly, which I'd never done before.

"Hey," I said. "It's me. Zee." My voice was a shaky whisper.

"What's wrong?" he said.

"Nothing."

"Then why are you—"

"Does something have to be wrong for me to call?" I said.

"I don't know. You just sound weird. You OK?"

Hearing his voice calmed me down. We didn't talk about much. School, mostly. Music a little. Five minutes on the phone and I was OK again. The bad feeling was gone.

"All right, well I should finish up the laundry before my dad gets home."

"Sure. See you in Bio."

I hung up and took a deep breath. Wherever my panic had come from, it was gone now, back like a snake crawling into its secret hole.

Sixteen

RELLY CALLED HIS MOM by her first name, which was Tannis. I found out later that she changed it from something normal back in the olden days. But her name wasn't the strangest thing about her.

"Why don't you sit down here for a second?" she said as I headed through the kitchen for the stairs.

"The guys are all—"

"Sit down." It wasn't exactly a command. But she wasn't asking politely, either. "We need to talk."

So I leaned my case against the wall and joined her at the kitchen table.

"Jonathan called. He'll be late." That was Butt's real name. Jonathan Vincent Butterfield.

Tannis had a trippy kind of feel about her. I don't mean she'd fried her brains with acid in the olden days. And she wasn't one of those have-a-nice-day granola types. Mood rings, wheat grass, tarot cards, yoga.

That kind of stuff wasn't big with her.

The only thing that fit with the old hippie ways was how deep she was into zodiac stuff. There was a picture of Aquarius in every room. The best one hung in the kitchen. It showed a girl pouring water from a clay jar. And even though it looked like something from the ancient days, it was a photo, not a painting. The girl had beautiful hair and was wearing a loose kind of dress belted with a piece of silver rope. She looked out at me from the picture with the same trancey gaze that Tannis wore right there and then.

Tannis offered me tea, which was kind of strange. Jolt and Mountain Dew: yeah. And Panther Blood, the stuff Relly found at the old Italian market. I got used to that. But tea was something I hardly ever drank. And it turned out to be this nasty, poxy-smelling stuff brewed out of roots and berries.

"Relly says you're good."

"I guess."

"There's never been a girl in any of his bands before. You know that, don't you?"

"Sure. But I don't think that—"

She cut me off. "What you think about Relly is not important. I'm more concerned with what you feel."

I sat there, not talking, figuring she'd get to the point soon enough.

And she did. "You know it's just me and Relly here.

That's the way it's always been. And his band has always practiced here. That was my idea. Did he tell you that? I helped him clear out the space in the attic."

She was staring at me with those big, accusing eyes. "Relly is not like other boys. Do you understand that? He is different. And he needs a place where he is safe. Where nobody will lead him astray."

"Look, I'm just the bass player, OK? That's all. I'm not leading anybody anywhere."

"Yes," Tannis said. Then we were quiet for a little while. I stared down at the gray-green leaves floating in my teacup. I could feel her eyes on me, accusing me of something, but I didn't know what.

"Zee?"

"Yeah?" I didn't meet her stare.

"I want you to promise me something."

This was getting way too weird. I just wanted to play. That's all.

"Will you promise me that no matter what happens, no matter what you see or hear or find out, you'll keep it to yourself? Relly is all I have. It's always been just the two of us. Do you promise me that everything you learn stays here? He likes you, Zee. And he doesn't like many people. He says you're good. He says he can trust you. Do you promise you'll keep it that way?"

Just then Butt came blundering into the kitchen.

"Hey, I just heard a good one. What's brown and sounds like a bell?"

It didn't occur to him that neither Tannis nor I was in the mood for his stupid jokes.

"Dung!" he said, making his voice ring like a Chinese gong. "Get it? Get it? Dung!"

He headed upstairs.

When his clomping had dwindled to nothing, Tannis said, "Promise."

"OK, sure. I promise." I got up. "We done?"

She said, "I'm going to hold you to that promise. Do you understand?"

No, I didn't. But I wanted to be out of there real bad. So I nodded.

"All right. I've said my piece. Go on now. They're waiting for you."

Seventeen

The next day we had a new bio teacher. Actually he was the old one, but he'd been out on sick leave since September. So the long-term sub was gone and Mr. Knacke was back.

He had that evil old-man smell, kind of sour and dry, like old coffee breath and mothballs and burning dust. He wasn't big. Still, when he came in the room, you sure knew he was there. And he wasn't ugly. Not exactly. But even at eight fifteen in the morning, his bald spot was shining bright red through his combover. And he had those little webs of white goo in the corners of his mouth.

"My name is Mr. Knacke. That's pronounced Kuh-Nack-ee. Do I make myself understood? Festus B. Knacke. Say it! All of you, say it! Now."

The whole bio class repeated his name, like we were in Marine boot camp and he was the drill sergeant.

"You!" He was talking, or I guess I should say, growling, at me. "What is your name?"

"Me?" It was kind of a shock, him picking me out of the crowd. Usually, keeping my mouth shut and my head down is safe. The nail that sticks up gets hammered flat. That's what my dad says.

"Yes, you." He put so much disgust into those two little words. "What is your name?"

I told him.

He stared at me like I was making some dumb joke. "Zee? Your name is Zee?"

"Yeah." What did he want? Should I explain it, or say I was sorry that my name was so weird? I just slunk deeper into my chair and he moved on to harass another kid.

Eighteen

"LORD CROT ALMIGHTY," Relly moaned. "I thought he was never coming back."

"You know him?"

"Do I know him? He was the scumpack who gave me an F last year in bio. You're in serious trouble. It took him a while to hate my guts. It looks like with you it's hate at first sight."

"But why? What did I do?"

"Didn't have to do anything. It's just the way it works with Knacke. He's the worst, Zee. I thought he was too sick to go on teaching. I heard some kids say he had cancer."

Butt scowled. "I heard other kids say he *is* cancer." We were standing in front of a bulletin board promoting "good mental hygiene."

"He really is nuts," Relly said. "If he didn't have—what do you call it, tenure?—they'd lock him up in the state looney hospital. You know how I found out I flunked bio last year?"

"How would I know that?"

"I was sitting in the kitchen. Somehow Knacke figured

out when I'd be alone. This was right after finals last June. I heard a car horn and looked out the window into the darkness. When I stuck my head out the front door, I heard a noise, like a balloon popping.

"The driveway exploded. A huge big letter F was burning on the blacktop. The car horn started up again. You know, real loud and crazy. Then it stopped for a second, and Knacke yelled, 'There's your grade, loser-boy!'

"My big F burnt itself out pretty fast. I stood there staring, like I wasn't even sure if I'd really seen it. Or if Knacke's craziness had rubbed off on me. His car started up, honking again, and he drove away."

As his story got weirder, I wonder if Relly was making the whole thing up. And if he was, then why? "This is for real?" I said.

He didn't answer. He just smiled and finished up the story.

"I went out and looked at the driveway. The scumpack had used some kind of lighter fluid that burnt but left no mark on the blacktop. Nobody but me had seen the fire. But standing there, I could still smell the smoke. Kind of sour and sweet at the same time.

"There was my final grade for bio. A burning F. 'See you next year!' That's what he yelled as he drove off."

Nineteen

So bio turned into a daily dose of torture.

Mr. Knacke had three or four different voices, as if there was a gang of Knackes inside him. Most of the time it was a flat droning noise, like an airplane heard from way far away. But sometimes it would explode into a screechy, scratchy yell, and he'd aim every kind of insult at the kids he called the "flat-liners." After he asked you a question, he'd make this beeping sound, like one of those machines in Intensive Care. And if you got it wrong, which was most of the time, then he'd buzz out the words "Brain dead! Brain dead!"

Once, when he passed back a really bad test, he stapled job applications from McDonald's on the ones that got Fs. "Would you like fries with that? Go on," he said, leaning in toward me so close I could smell him. "Try it! Say it, because that's where you'll be for the rest of your life."

I put up with it. What else could I do?

Like there was a girl called Michelle Eckers, who was born with one leg shorter than the other. And she had to clomp around or else wear these spasmo-looking shoes. And everybody knew. And some kids made fun of her, of course. But what could she do? Complaining wouldn't make her leg any longer. And what could I do about Mr. Knacke? Complaining wouldn't make him lay off with the insults and ranting and extra work.

So I did my time at school. And as soon as I could, I was out of there and back to Relly's house for more hard guitar slag and slippery bass groan.

Twenty

"IT'S A REAL GIG," Relly announced. "The all-ages show at Waterstreet. There's five other bands and we have to go second. But we'll burn the place down. When we're done, there won't be anything left but smoke and ashes."

We only had a week to get ready. So we had to get the set list together fast, narrowing the songs down to a half-hour set. The big question was, Do we do any covers? We could do Zeppelin and Priest and AC/DC. But we also had original tunes. Relly's and mine.

Just a couple of days before the gig, we'd written our first tune together. Jerod had taken off at about eleven, driving back to his nice big house in Pittsford. Butt stuck around. He had nowhere to go, and nobody at home who cared how late he stayed out. And I knew my dad was working till close that night.

So we banged out the new tune. Relly's black surging riffs and my words. It was called "Ten Thousand Charms."

And all three of us agreed that we had to do the tune when we played out the first time.

"That's it," Relly said when we finally got the tune where we wanted it. Sometimes I thought the sound went on forever, up there in the shadows and weird peaks of attic roofline. Echoes above our heads. The traces of lost chords, broken riffs, whispers and screams.

"That's it. That's the sound I kept hearing in my head." He had that strange look again, half mystic and half maniac. "This song is the real Ghost Metal," he whispered. "Till right now, till tonight, it was just in my head. But now it's out. It's finally really in the world."

It was important to him that I understood what he meant by *ghost*. It wasn't cheap booga-booga horror or little kids on Halloween in old sheets. "Uh-uh," Relly said. "*Ghost* is the old word for spirit. Like Holy Ghost. Spirit, not stupid scary-movie crot."

Butt shrugged. I guess he'd heard this routine before.

I said, "OK, so we do the tune?"

"Yeah. We do it last in the set. And we leave 'em all shaking and gasping for breath."

Butt gave his bass drum a couple of powerful kicks. That was his way of saying "Count me in, all the way."

"All right. We'll run it tomorrow with Jerod," Relly said. "And it'll be ready for Sunday."

Twenty-one

THE NEXT DAY, while we were doing some kind of idiot worksheet about blastulas and gastrulas, Mr. Knacke came down my aisle and caught a glimpse of a logo I'd drawn in my notebook. Scorpio Bone—in kind of spiky letters, like the name was made out of hunks of broken glass.

"What, pray tell, is Scorpio Bone?"

"It's a band," I said, feeling his invisible noose slip around my neck.

"What kind of music do they play?"

"Ghost Metal." The noose tightened.

"Is that so? Someone is clearly an imbecile." That was his favorite word. *Imbecile*. He said it like a Nazi general reaming out his flunkies. "Scorpions are arachnids. They do not have bones."

"Yeah, I know. It's just a name."

Some kids were snickering now, because they knew it was me and Relly's band. And the word had gone around that we were doing the all-ages show at Waterstreet that Sunday.

"That's moronic. Whoever came up with that name is a moron. And I suppose you're even more of a moron for thinking it so worthy that you'd draw it on your belongings."

I didn't say a thing. I could barely breathe. The noose pulled up hard and I knew he was going to keep on tightening it.

Twenty-two

WE HAD ONE LAST practice before the show. "It's OK," Relly said, "that's the way it usually goes."

We'd sounded awful. Out of tune, out of sync, weak and unsure. "It's OK. If you sound too good before a show, that's always bad luck."

But I had some serious doubts. If I couldn't remember the changes to the tunes, we'd wander all over the place. If Jerod couldn't keep the words straight, we'd look like wanks, stupid amateurs. And we'd be standing there in front of a couple hundred kids. Even Butt, who was usually solid as a cement block, had seemed to lose it.

"I don't know," I said. "Maybe we should forget this. You really think we're ready?"

This was the first time I'd seen Relly mad. "What are you talking about? We don't have any choice here. We're playing tomorrow and it's got to be perfect." When things got bad, Relly's voice got quieter, not louder.

"OK, OK," I said. He didn't exactly scare me. I mean, it wasn't like when my dad got all furious and went around the house breaking things. But I couldn't look Relly in the eye. I couldn't stand being there with him right then.

"I'll see you tomorrow," I said, grabbing the set list and my case and heading for the door.

Twenty-three

WE SHOWED UP ON time, but of course everything took twice as long as it should have. Because there were five bands to get on and off in a couple hours, everyone had to use the same basic setup. Drums, amps, mikes. This was a pain, because we weren't used to the gear. But those were the rules.

They said we'd have a sound check. That was a joke. We stood on the stage for about five minutes before the sound man even noticed us there. And when we asked questions or said the levels in the monitors were too low, he didn't even bother to answer.

So it was looking pretty grizzly as the doors opened for the crowd. I was hoping nobody would show up. Then at least we wouldn't look like wanks in front of the whole world. No such luck. Some of the other bands had a pretty good following. And by the time things got rolling, the place was packed.

From where we were hiding, off to the side of the stage, Waterstreet looked even bigger than before. Hundreds and hundreds of kids were all milling around. Shouts, screams, laughter, arguments, greetings, and just plain talking. Even without the bands playing, it was way loud.

I didn't have butterflies in my stomach. It was more like a swarm of sharks churning around. My palms were sweaty. My legs were weak. And we weren't even on yet.

"Look," Relly said. "No matter what happens, we're still the best. Right? Doesn't matter what this crowd thinks. If they like us, fine. If they don't, that's fine too. We're still the best."

Jerod was all hyped up, and I guess he'd never looked better. Maybe being nervous was a good thing. He was practically glowing with excitement, talking about nothing, doing high-fives, kind of jumping around and dancing. Butt was silent. He kept looking at me as though he thought I was the weak link and if we messed up, the whole disaster would be my fault. Relly stroked his fingers over the fretboard of his Strat, like he was trying to calm the guitar down.

Then the first band went on. The crowd was screaming already. And I knew I didn't have long before it all was over.

It was impossible, at least for me, to really listen to the

first band. I mean I heard them. I knew they were playing. But I was so nervous I couldn't pay any attention.

I guess they were all right. The crowd seemed to like them. But nobody really listens to the opening act.

They did their last tune, which sounded to me like a retread of Sabbath's "Paranoid." And then we were on.

Twenty-four

IT STARTED OUT OK. We were pretty together on "Hole in the Sky." Butt was solid. No matter how scared he was, he kept us together that day. And I was OK, too. Relly stretched out a little on the second tune. And Jerod finally got his stride on "Blood Drive," yelling and wailing and shaking like a wild man.

I kept my eyes pretty much on the Ibanez. There was no way I could look out at the crowd without melting down to nothing. I stayed with Butt, laying down the heavy bottom. I played off of Relly, doubling lines, snaking around his riffs. And I listened to Jerod through the monitors, especially on the words I had written. It was so weird to hear them that big, that strong, blasting out over a couple hundred kids.

We had three songs to go when the Ghost Metal thing started to happen.

The crowd was with us. We might not have been the top of the bill. But they heard what we could do. And they were starting to like it. Relly finally shook off the fear and let himself go. I glanced over at Butt and now he, too, was pouring himself totally into the noise.

So I guess I was ready at last. I was safe there on the stage. Which is very weird. Safe even though everyone was looking at us. I was free too, which is even stranger. Free to make the biggest throb in the world.

We tore through "The Ocean," the old Led Zeppelin tune. And the crowd was screaming. We went right into "Scar Monkey," and as Relly laid on the riff hard and heavy, I finally heard his Ghost Metal thing. We were loud, huge, strong as a thunderhead. And still, inside the monstrous noise I swear I could hear this ringing silence.

I looked over at him and he gave me one nod. That was all. He nodded as if to say, "Yeah, that's it, that's the sound." The song rose like a sea monster out of some churning waves. The crowd went crazy, guys banging their heads against the invisible wall and girls glowing as the spotlights swept over them. And I went into that empty secret place, just me and Relly.

And then we were on our last tune, "Ten Thousand Charms." We ground like huge millstones squeezing out lightning and thunder. It was better than ever. It was the best we'd ever sounded.

The most amazing thing was to hear my words roaring out of the huge PA system. I'd kept those words secret, bottled up, for a long time. And now Jerod, beautiful Jerod, was wailing them for a couple hundred kids.

The crowd loved it. Or maybe they loved us. I don't know. It's all a jumble in my head. Did they hear the Ghost Metal silence, too? The roar and the nothingness inside the roar? Did they hear my words? I mean really hear them? I don't know. Did they get the feverish, swelling buzz like us? Who's to say?

But they sure made noise when we were done. They yelled and clapped and whistled and some were pushing up against the stage, like they wanted to touch Relly or Jerod. Like we had some magic that maybe might rub off.

I could hardly look at the crowd, it was so intense. I wanted to run, to escape all those surging bodies and crashing waves of noise. Jerod loved it, prancing around, accepting the applause. And Butt was thrilled, too, wearing a big doofy smile.

And Relly? I figured this would be his moment. I thought he'd stay onstage for as long as they'd let him, soaking up the good feeling.

But he was gone.

The next couple of minutes were all a blur. The MC came out and was hyping up the crowd for the next act. I think Jerod threw himself off the stage and was sucked into the crowd. Butt gave us a last blast of drumstick dynamite and headed backstage.

But where was Relly?

I followed Butt to the so-called dressing room. It was chaos. Four other bands were there, and some kids had snuck in from the crowd. People were yelling and swaggering around, chugging Mountain Dew, joking, huddling in little clusters, eating pizza, and acting like a pack of maniacs.

No sign of Relly, however.

His Strat was in its case, so I knew he'd come through the dressing room. But why had he run off so fast?

I cornered Butt and said, "Where'd he go? Why'd he take off?"

"Down that way," a girl wearing way too much purple mascara told me. "I think I saw him go down the back hall."

Twenty-five

SO I WENT. I followed.

The hallway was long and dim, with about a thousand band names scrawled on the concrete walls. The back door was open. Outside was an alley. A couple of dumpsters and a stack of black plastic garbage bags. Two kids were hanging around there, smoking.

"Did you see Relly?" I asked.

"Who?"

Running out of the alley, I had a choice. Left or right on this empty back street. I kept asking myself, *Why do I need to find him?* What was the big deal? If he wanted to run off, that was his business, right?

It was one of those cold, hard, early winter days when the sunset painted the whole sky red. In one direction was the burning glow. In the other was shadow.

I ran with the sunset at my back. This was a section of the city I didn't know. And on a Sunday afternoon, it was empty, even desolate. *How can I possibly find him?* I kept asking myself. *And why?* He ran off for a good reason. If he wanted to be with us, with me, he would have stayed at Waterstreet.

Still, I ran. Still, somehow I followed his path.

The sky was now all crimson, writhing and swirling with sunset fire.

I stopped at the entrance to a narrow alley. More trash cans, more piles of broken-down boxes. More blank, empty back doors.

And there he was, huddled like a wounded animal.

I hurried toward him. "Relly, what's wrong? What are you doing?"

"You shouldn't be here," he whispered.

"What are you talking about?"

The light from the sky was amazing, making everything red. My hands, his face, even the wet pavement.

"You're not ready," he said.

"I don't get it," I said, kneeling down beside him. "What's wrong?"

He took off his coat, then started fumbling to pull his shirt over his head.

"What are you doing?" I was helpless with him in this state. Maybe he was crazy and what can you do with a crazy person but stand there and watch? Maybe he was sick, and I should be running to call an ambulance. Or maybe I was crazy and sick, and none of this was really happening.

His hand flickered. I mean the skin looked like it was moving, all melting and misty. The whole alleyway was drenched in the sky's red throb.

"Go away," he moaned. "You're not ready."

He got his shirt off and he looked so thin and weak.

"Relly, listen to me. I'm going to call——"

"No!" he hissed. "Nobody else. Nobody can see." Then he took hold of my hand. His felt hot. Not like fevered flesh but like something right out of the oven.

"Relly, you're sick. You stay right here and I'll call——"

Then I saw the first little glint of fire. And now I was sure I was the crazy one. Flame doesn't just appear on a boy's skin, right? Fire doesn't come from a body.

But still, I saw it. Red and orange tongues of flame rising from Relly, like he was coated with gasoline and I'd tossed a lit match on him. I saw the flames rise up, swirling and rushing. "Get away!" he moaned. "Get back!"

I wanted to hold onto him, to hold back the flame. But it hurt too much. And so I fell back as he stood, completely covered in fire.

Someone was screaming. Me? Maybe. Relly? Maybe. Both of us? I don't know.

I grabbed a hunk of old discarded carpet to smother the fire. "No." The voice came, from him or from the flame. "Don't."

He stood before me burning from head to toe. Black

smoke poured upward, a strange, almost perfumey smoke. He raised his hands over his head like a conqueror, the winner of some deadly fight. A minute before, he looked weak and sick. Now he was beautiful and fearsome. Flames roared out of him, and I knelt there on the cold wet pavement, sure I'd gone totally insane.

I guess I was crying now. Somebody was, and I don't think it was Relly. I closed my eyes, trying to make the fire go away. But I could still hear it. And still feel it burning on my face.

Just as fast as it came, it went away. The heat dwindled. And the red glow I could see through my closed eyes vanished, too. No more uprushing noise. "Relly?" I said, still not looking.

He was dead for sure. How could he survive that? I'd knelt there weak and useless while Relly had burned to nothing.

"Relly?" When I finally opened my eyes, he was wearing his long coat again. But his feet were bare, and what I could see of his legs, too. He looked exhausted, totally used up. Still, he was alive.

"Now you know," he whispered.

I came toward him, afraid it would start all over again.

"Now you know what I truly am."

The sunset was gone and long, cold shadows were filling the alley. Relly pulled his coat tighter to his chest.

"Now there's no turning back. You know about me and soon enough you'll know about yourself."

fire   earth   wind   water

Part Two

One

YEAH, IT STARTS WITH FIRE.

Relly was the Burning Boy. And I guess that made me the Crazy Girl. Because I believed it. I mean, I never once doubted what I saw that day. He was standing in an alley in a cloak of fire. A minute later it was over. He was OK. Totally exhausted, too weak to even talk. But not a burn mark on him. No sign of the flames that had poured out of his body.

I wrapped him up in his coat, and I sat with him a long time, holding on.

Then I got him over to Clinton Avenue and we took the bus back to his house. Late on Sundays there's hardly anybody riding buses. So it was like we had our own private route. The driver was in a trance after going back and forth across the city all day. He didn't even notice Relly had no shoes on. Outside was dark and cold. Inside was too brightly lit. The buzz of the lights hurt Relly. I could feel it. We sat in the very back, huddled together, not saying a word.

He'd tell me when it was the right time. I knew that. I'd find out everything. But riding back home on the bus, we didn't say a word.

Only as I helped him up his steps did I break the silence. "I'll go back and get the gear. Is there anything besides the Strat?"

He shook his head. "It was real, Zee," he said, like he heard the question without me saying it out loud. "It's real. It happened before. And it'll happen again."

"Yeah, I know. So I'm not insane."

He shrugged. "Sane or insane. Doesn't make much difference now. It's real."

Two

MY DAD HAD OFF that night. But I headed straight to my room and didn't even see him. He was downstairs reading, I guess.

I lay in bed for a long time replaying what had gone on that day.

It seemed like I had two choices. One was to deny everything. I could just say I was totally freaked out by the show, stressed way into the Crazy Zone. Playing out for the first time. The crowds of screaming kids. Relly's Ghost Metal pouring from the amps. My words big as thunder. Maybe I was sick too, feverish again, which always makes my brain work in strange ways. Maybe it was all in my head.

Or I could accept it. I could say to myself, "All right, Relly explodes into flames sometimes. That's just the way he is."

I had an old record called *Everything You Know Is Wrong,* by this acid-head comedy group called the

Firesign Theatre. I listened to it once, after my uncle Otho had broken up his record collection and given it to me. I guess it was supposed to be funny. But it just seemed strange to me. I didn't understand a lot of it. The story line wandered all over the place and I didn't laugh once at any of the jokes. Exactly the kind of weirdness that Uncle Otho would love. I stuck it away in the attic, but the name of the record kept coming back to me.

"Everything You Know Is Wrong." I said it out loud, lying there in bed.

If metalhead freak boys can explode into flame, then what else was possible? In a way, that was much scarier than accepting what my eyes had seen. One totally bizarro thing is bad enough. But if that could happen, then what else was waiting for me?

I usually kept my thoughts pretty much under control, like they were wild animals and I was in charge of the zoo. Yeah, I might obsess about a burning car wreck or the coils in the electric heater. But that's as far as it went. And maybe all my obsessing was even a way to keep the other stuff locked up in nice dark cages.

So lying there in bed, it really scared me what might come crawling out of my brain.

What if Relly told me that everybody bursts into flame now and then?

What if Mr. Perfect Jerod said he wanted to be my boyfriend?

What if my dad understood that I needed a real father and not just somebody who paid the bills and left supper in the fridge for me?

What if I was the best bass player in the universe?

What if Tannis could put spells on people the way pagan priestesses did in the olden days?

What if Relly and me were together forever?

That one really scared me. So I got out a candle and lit it. And sat there watching the flame, which sometimes works to calm me down.

Only that night it didn't work. In fact, it made the feeling even worse. The little flame seemed dangerous, or maybe a warning of danger. Anything was possible now. Anything, good or bad, real or unreal. My skin was hot and damp with sweat. My thoughts were all a blur, one idea melting into the next. I saw Relly on fire and a couple hundred screaming faces. I saw the back alley, filled with red sunset light.

This was too much. So I blew out the candle and went down the hall to the bathroom. Without really thinking why, I started the water in the tub.

Our house is old and sometimes that can be a pain. The windows are drafty and the floors squeak. But if my dad ever gets around to redoing the place, I'll fight him to the death to keep the old bathtub. It's big, and it's got those claw feet holding it off the floor. And I can fit in it all the way, stretch out, and be totally under the surface.

So I ran a bath for myself, real hot, and soon I was submerged. Only then did the bad feeling go away. I stayed under as long as I could, then came up gasping and went below again. Eyes closed, hugging myself, holding my breath, all the world went away. I was safe underwater, perfect and secret.

And the fever was gone too. Finally, the damp smoldering in my body had stopped.

Three

WHEN I SAW RELLY the next day, it was like we'd both done something really wrong and didn't want to bring it up. I'd heard girls talking about going to a party and getting drunk and sneaking off with some boy. And the next day they kept to themselves, not sure who saw them the night before or what they'd seen.

I guess it was like that with me and Relly. We hadn't done anything wrong. Nothing at all. In fact, lots of kids were friendlier now, as the word got around about our show and how Scorpio Bone blew the other bands off the stage. Still, we didn't say much to each other.

He even made up some bogus excuse why he couldn't eat lunch with me that day.

Then we were in bio again together and we got to see the Full Knacke.

He had this thing about smoking. He hated it, I mean, truly hated it with all the hate inside him. And so he built this smoking machine he called the Marlboro Man with glass tubes for lungs. It had been a full-size lifesaving dummy, but now it breathed all by itself, the air sucked in by a bellows run on a little electric motor. That day, Knacke set him up and put a cigarette in his mouth.

He lit a match, snarling through his teeth, "Welcome to Marlboro Country." He got the pump going and we had to sit for twenty minutes watching the black goo collect in the glass tubes. Knacke was getting all excited, saying, "See? See the filth you're taking into your bodies? Do you understand? If you smoke, then you pollute yourselves." And he made us come up, row by row, and look real close.

The dummy had a cowboy hat and Knacke would show us ads from magazines. "You see him? Do you understand what happened to this imbecile? He smoked himself to death." Knacke passed the ads around. Tough-looking cowboys. Macho range-riders. "Dead of cancer!" Knacke would scream at us. "Dead from smoking!"

I think he'd won some kind of award from the American Cancer Society. And the school loved it, of course. Somebody in Admin put up a display on the bulletin board right by the front door. "Festus B. Knacke, fighting for the lives of our young people."

We had bio last period. He'd done the smoking bit for all his classes. So by the end of the day, the lungs were pretty disgusting.

Four

PRACTICE WAS STRANGE the next day. Jerod was totally cranked up from the show, rattling on about how great we were and how we'd be headlining soon. Butt was excited, too, I guess. Only, unlike Jerod, he noticed that something was wrong.

In the beginning, it was just Butt and Relly. In some ways they couldn't have been more different. Butt was built like a caveman, all muscle and shaved boney head. Relly wasn't exactly frail. He could stand up in the blast from the amps and I think it even made him stronger. Still, he was no ironman. Butt wasn't what you'd call smart either. And sometimes the stuff Relly talked about went way over his head.

All the same, they were the core of the band. They'd been together the longest and Butt could tell when things weren't right for Relly.

I stayed in my place, off to the side. Jerod jumped around and practically strangled the mike stand. Butt drove the band like a thudding train engine. And Relly played stuff I'd never heard before.

No chord charts that night. No words for Jerod. Just a huge endless riff like a monster snake slithering out of its nowhere hole. And just when I thought we'd gotten to the end, Relly took us deeper and farther.

He looked over at me, gave a little nod. Was it noise that came out of the amps then? Yeah, I guess. Was it music? Yeah, that too. But it was something else. If I'd been one of the Dungeons & Dragons crowd, I might have said Relly was doing sorcery. If I'd read a lot of elves and dwarves stuff or hung out with the Wicca girls, I'd say he was casting a spell.

But I wasn't. So I just thought, *All right, he's opening the door. And I guess we're all going through.*

What door? I didn't know then. Where were we going? It would take me a while to figure that out, too.

Did I want to go with him? Oh yeah. No question about that. Butt and Jerod did, too, though I guess they couldn't see it the way I did. Butt just drubbed his drums. And Jerod wailed and practiced looking good, riding the riff. We all went though, in our ways. Relly opened the door and Scorpio Bone headed straight through.

OK, I know this sounds like I was going crazy. But sometimes the truth is crazy. Sometimes everything you know *is* wrong. And you've got to face that straight on if you want to really live your life. I was in the band and I was staying. Relly was my best friend and there was no way I'd do anything to change that. I was heading for the "other side," as Relly called it. And there was no turning back.

Five

THE NEXT DAY, Knacke hooked up a dead frog to a hand-cranked magneto and had us work it. One at a time we'd come up to the front of the class and take hold of the sweaty black crank. Round and round till electric current was pouring out the wires and into the frog.

It twitched and spazzed there on the table, like it was halfway back from the land of the dead. Some kids were seriously grossed out. Some thought it was pretty cool.

"In the earliest days of science," Knacke told us, "it was thought that living creatures could be brought back to life by the use of electric current."

It was my turn to go up and work the crank. "There it is, Zee." I hated when he said my name. "There it is up close and personal." I turned the crank and watched the frog thrash around. He was dead. Sure. But he was alive too, in some weird way. His rubbery lips came apart and his tongue stuck out.

The worst part was when his eyes slid open and he lay

there staring at me. I looked away. Knacke had come close and was giving me the same dead-alive stare as the frog.

"Don't be afraid," Knacke whispered to me. "There's nothing to fear."

I thought I was going to throw up. Letting go of the magneto crank, I stood there in front of the whole class like an idiot. Some kids were snickering and making jokes. Gary Geetz, who always thought everything terrible was funny, said something about "love at first sight."

"Shut up, Geetz," I said. "Shut your big fat mouth."

That was all it took. I got detention. Just me and Knacke and his Marlboro Man.

Six

USUALLY, DETENTION WASN'T so bad. I figured I could waste a couple of hours doing homework. Or I could blow that off and sit and draw band logos and write new lyrics in my special notebook.

But detention with Knacke was different. He actually made you work. And he only had one kid at a time.

My job was to clean out the Marlboro Man's disgusting lungs. Soap suds. A wire brush. A sink full of black gunk.

I held the tubes up to the light, one at a time.

"Not clean enough. Not by a long shot," Knacke said, glaring at the tubes.

Alone with him, I got a solid whiff of his smell. Even with the cigarette goo and the nasty soap, I could smell the stinking essence. It wasn't pit stink, though sometimes his shirts got pretty dark under the arms. It wasn't unwashed clothes. Or liquor, like Mr. Bittmeyer. Or cheap deodorant, like every football player there ever was.

No, it was more like a dead animal. That's the closest thing to his stench. Something that had been dead for a while.

"I've been looking forward to this little time together," he said, leaning in close. Grabbing one of the tubes, he gave it a good rinse. He nodded, and I went on to the next one.

"We're well aware of your friendship with Relly."

My hands went kind of dead. I watched the water run out of the faucet. I listened to the millions of little soap bubbles popping.

"He's not like the other students here, is he?" His voice changed, like somebody else was talking through his mouth. "Nor are you. That's quite plain to see. We know everything there is to know about you."

Maybe I should've just run out. No doubt about it, I'd be in even worse trouble. I thought real hard about it, picturing myself tearing down the hall with Knacke behind yelling.

But no, I just sat there and waited.

Knacke watched me, waiting for my reaction. When I said nothing, and did nothing, he smiled his big shiny bogus grin. "Since I've been back, I've had my eye on the two of you. And before then too."

I kept my mouth closed. He was toying with me, trying to get me to squirm. I just stood there, waiting.

"You're not like the others. That's quite apparent."

Still I kept silent, like I was a good soldier getting tortured but telling no secrets.

He shrugged after a while, as if I was making him sad. "Perhaps another time you'll want to talk more. We have so much to discuss." Then he put back on his plastic smile. "You're excused now. I can finish up."

He took the bottle brush and I was out the door with my hands still dripping black ooze.

Seven

I GOT A CALL the next day at home.

"Hey," a gritty voice said. "How you doing?"

"Who is this?"

"Who do you think?"

For a second I was afraid it was Knacke. *He's not only the king of evil scumpacks at school,* I thought, *he's a pervert too, calling girls at home.* But I was wrong.

"I was at Waterstreet. I saw your show. All the girls were hot for Jerod and Relly. But I was watching you."

"That's just great. Now what do you want?"

He kind of laughed, but it sounded mean and dirty too. "What are you doing?" he asked.

"Listening to some slimeball on the phone."

"Funny. Real funny."

"What do you want?" I asked.

"Just to talk. Get to know you better."

"Well I don't know who you are. And I don't want to know. So goodbye." I hung up. The phone rang again. "Die, all right? Why don't you just die?"

"Zee, what's going on?" It was my dad. "You answer the phone with 'die' now?"

"Some pervo was harassing me a minute ago. I didn't know it was you."

"Well, I'm just calling to say I'll be late tonight. I'm going out with Donna Lee after work, all right?"

"Sure, whatever."

Two seconds after I hung up with my dad, the phone rang again.

I picked it up but didn't say a thing. Neither did he, whoever he was. We played a game of chicken, seeing who'd hang up first. Silence stretched, and stretched even thinner. I could feel him on the other end, even if I couldn't hear a thing. I think the silence was even worse than his voice. But I didn't back down. I didn't say a word.

I won the game. He hung up after a while. I won, but it didn't make me feel any better.

Eight

WE WERE IN THE attic, just the two of us. The wind was moaning in the eaves. Wet snow spattered the tiny windows.

"I got a call last night."

"Yeah?" Relly said.

"It was some sicko. He said he saw our show at Waterstreet. I hung up on him."

"Enemies. They're gathering."

"What are you talking about?"

"Soon, soon. When you're ready, you'll know."

I was scared and angry. And I'd had enough of his mystery talk. "This is so stupid!" I yelled at him. "What is it with all these secrets?"

Only then did he look right at me. "After what you saw, you've got to ask me that?"

"I didn't see anything."

"Now who's being stupid?" he asked.

"All right, all right. I saw you burst into flames and

a minute later you were perfectly OK. Is that what you want me to say?"

"Well, is it true or isn't it?"

"I don't know!" I shouted.

"Yes, you do," he whispered back.

We were quiet a long time, listening to the wind coil around the house, slow and powerful as a boa constrictor.

It was like we were playing the same stupid game as I had on the phone. Who would talk first? Who would give up and break the dead air between us?

As it turned out, we both won that night. Or maybe we both lost.

Butt came clomping up the steps.

He banged the door open and announced, "I got a great idea. How about a song called 'Message from Uranus'? That would be cool, right? You could write the words." He was looking at me. "Like a science fiction thing only it's about Uranus, get it? Your anus! Get it?"

"Yeah, I get it," I said. "Maybe later."

He climbed behind his set and got both his feet going, whaling the kick drums fast and loud. That was the way he showed he was happy. Laughing, sure. Still, that pounding kick-drum roll was the real sound of Butt's delight.

Nine

THE BEST RUMOR about Knacke, or, I guess, the worst one, was about the dog's head. I heard different versions. But it always had to do with some dog that barked too much down the street from Knacke's house. So he lured it over, or went in the middle of the night and grabbed it. "And he cut off the head and he's got it floating in a bucket of chemicals." That's how kids usually finished the story. "It's been alive for years, floating there all hooked up to tubes."

Somehow he figured out a way to keep the dog's head alive and somewhere in his basement he still had it. A big black cauldron. A glass bowl. A vat. Different stories had different details. Tubes into the neck. Or up the nose. Floating in clear chemical broth. Or bubbling green goo.

So when it got really bad in bio class, I thought maybe I'd end up like the dog. I mean, I knew that teachers didn't usually kill kids and cut off their heads, but sometimes it felt like that was the next step after detention.

I was there in the bio classroom again, just me and Knacke.

For three days straight I hadn't done any homework. So he told me I had to stay late.

He had everything set up for me when I arrived. The Marlboro Man's lungs were fine this time. So instead of scouring tubes, I was supposed to completely clean out a big glass display case. Inside was something ten times grosser than tobacco lungs. It was an old piece of meat that maggots had been eating for a week. I guess he was trying to show cycles of nature. You know, how everything returns to the earth and the plants and animals use it up. But this wasn't a little compost pile with carrot peelings and dead leaves. No, Knacke went straight for the gross-out. A hunk of meat all swarmed over with white fly larvae.

"We're done with that project now," he said. "Take everything out, dispose of it, and then scrub the equipment."

I just stood there, staring.

"You see there the end of all flesh. All living creatures—from humans to worms—return to just such a state. Beyond death there is only decay. Do you understand?" He pointed. "Now clean it up."

I didn't move.

"Did you hear me?" he said.

"I'm not sticking my hand in there," I said.

"I didn't ask you. I told you. Now get to work." He wasn't exactly smiling, but I could tell he was enjoying this.

"No way. It's disgusting. Do it yourself." I didn't care what he did to me. A letter home, sending me down to the assistant principal's office for a yell-at from Frankengoon, suspension, even. "I'm not doing it."

He glared at me. When he got mad, his face looked shiny and swollen. His eyes were red around the edges, like a drunk's. And his breath came in panting sniffs.

"Get to work, young lady." He was holding a pair of rubber gloves.

I didn't take them. "Forget it," I said. "You can't make me do it."

He started into one of those "Who do you think you are?" speeches. But I'd made my choice and I wasn't backing down.

"Look," I said after a while. "What do you want from me? Just tell me why I'm the one you're picking on."

"Picking on? What do you mean? You show much promise. I merely hoped that a little discipline would turn you around. Make you a better student. Perhaps bring out your best qualities."

"You hated me the minute you saw me. I just need to know why."

"I don't hate anyone," he said. "I merely noted the

traits that set you apart. I want to see my students succeed to the best of—"

I headed for the door.

"Where do you think you're going?" he snarled.

"Home. You want to call Frankengoon and have me thrown out of school, fine. But I'm not putting up with this anymore."

"Get back here!"

I kept going.

Ten

THE SCHOOL WAS EMPTY at that hour. Endless ranks of lockers, shiny floors reflecting the red exit lights, a far-off hum.

I went straight for the main entrance. And even though I'd been going to that school for weeks, still I got kind of lost. I mean, I knew where I was, but it seemed like the distances were all wrong and the doors weren't where I expected.

It was dark in some of the hallways. A couple hours before, there were crowds of kids, yelling and talking and hanging around. Now it was like I was trapped in some Egyptian tomb and couldn't find my way out.

Turning around, I went back the way I'd come. Only I ended up in another hallway where one fluorescent light bulb was buzzing and throbbing with sickly white light.

Then I heard a metallic squeak. It came. It went. It came back. I don't know why, but I headed toward the sound.

I passed the main Admin suite, where Frankengoon had his office. Maybe it was him, rocking back and forth in his chair, squeaking up and down.

But then I found myself in the gym wing and thought, *It's somebody using the workout equipment. Weights or a Nautilus or a rowing machine.*

I went round the corner and saw the source of the squeak. It was a janitor, doing the floor. He stuck his mop in the squeezer and yanked down the handle. He moved real slow, like he was trying to get every drop of dirty water out of the mop.

As I came down the hall, he looked up and let go of the squeezer handle. "It's you," he said, and I felt a sick rising in my stomach. I'd never seen him before. Not that I paid much attention to janitors, but this one I would have remembered.

He was kind of hunched over, and his left eye seemed to be bigger than his right. When he talked, there was a hissing sound too, like air escaping from a tire. "You all done with our friend?"

"What are you—"

"Mr. Knacke," he murmured. "Our mutual friend." He set the mop down. A shiny slick covered a swath of the floor, like he was mopping with black coffee.

"Look, I just need to get home, OK? I'm all turned around. Which way is the main entrance?"

"What's your rush?" he said, straightening up as best he could. As he moved, light from behind shone on the dark wet floor. And I saw myself there, reflected, but all bent and smeary. "What do you got waiting for you at home, Zee?"

Hearing him say my name was way too freaky. I panicked, I guess. I had to get out of there and away from him. And so I ran. Fast.

Maybe I needed that jolt of cold fear. Because after seeing the guy with the mop, my mind was all clear and I went straight for the right doorway. It wasn't till I'd gotten off the school grounds, panting and trying to get my heart to slow down, that I realized where I'd heard that voice before. The guy with the mop was the disgusting guy on the phone the other night. He knew my name, he knew my number, and he knew where I lived.

Eleven

"OK, NOW YOU'RE GOING to tell me everything," I said. "What is going on, Relly? You've got to tell me."

We were walking along a gravel path in Mount Hope Cemetery. My first real date. Other girls get a movie and dinner. I got The Beautiful City of the Dead, as Relly called it. Other girls got small talk about school or TV or bands coming to town. Not me.

"We're gods," he said.

"Right. We're gods."

"I'm not kidding."

"I know you're not kidding," I said. "That's what scares me."

"It's true, Zee. You saw me. You saw the fire come, right? That was no lie."

"And I'm going to burst into flames, too? That's what you're going to tell me next, right?"

"No. Not flame. Not you."

"Then what are you talking about? Gods? I'm about as

godlike as a . . . as a . . .You're talking like a looney! You know that?"

"Just because you're looney doesn't mean you don't tell the truth."

We walked along, silent, for a while.

The cemetery really is a beautiful place, with winding paths and little ponds, hills overgrown with tall grass, endless ranks of gravestones. I didn't put up any fuss when he said he wanted for us to go there. I knew we could be alone there, just the two of us and a quarter million dead people. I like the quiet. I like the weeping maidens, angels, draped urns, crosses, and obelisks. I guess it was kind of romantic, even. Just the two of us, walking on a cold afternoon.

I'd brought along my notebook and copied down some of the gravestone poetry.

Weep not for me, my friends so dear.
I am not dead, just sleeping here.
My grassy bed, my grave you see.
Prepare in life to follow me.

"We're gods. Both of us," Relly said again after a while.

"You mean, like, I'm Venus and you're Jupiter?"

"Not planets, gods. The real thing. Gods that once were and will be again." I hated it when he talked this way. And I loved it too. Until that minute, scuffing through the dead leaves in Mount Hope, I would have just said I couldn't stand it when Relly talked like he was insane. But something had changed. In me maybe, in him, or in the whole world. I don't know. Whatever it was, it gave me a feeling like I'd never had before.

Right, me, the bass player hidden back behind Relly and Jerod. Right, the girl who never talked. I was a god. Me, Zee, lousy at school, sniffling with colds half my life, the one nobody noticed. I was a god now. Or maybe I always had been.

I wanted to laugh. And I guess if I'm being honest, I wanted to cry too. "It's all a lie," I whispered. "But go on, keep talking."

"It's not a lie. We've got the power, Zee. Real power like hardly anyone in the whole world. Gods don't die. Think about it, Zee. You'll never have to die."

We stopped, looking down on a pond in a little steep-sided valley. The water was utterly still and inky black. It was strange, what I felt. Peaceful and terrified at the same time. The quiet of the cemetery gave me a sense of peace. And Relly beside me, talking about gods, made me want to run and never turn back.

The strangest thing was not that I'd have these feelings, but that I'd have them at the same time. How could I hold such opposites in my heart? But I did. I hated Relly for the way he made me feel. And I never wanted to say goodbye. I loved being in the graveyard with him and I wanted to escape like a drowning swimmer wants air.

"OK, we're gods," I said. No point in arguing with him. He was so matter of fact. "So what does that mean?"

"First, we're not like everyone else."

That was almost funny. Me and Relly like other people? A couple of Ghost Metal kids on a date in the cemetery. How could anyone think that was normal?

"I mean that the same rules don't apply to us. Because we're gods."

"So I can skip school and I won't get in trouble? Secret gods don't have to take final exams?"

"I'm serious, Zee. Serious as a heart attack."

"All right. So we're different and the rules don't apply to us. What else?"

"They'll do anything to get what they want from us. From you."

"Who's they?" I asked.

"Knacke, for starters. And Frankengoon. He's part of it, too. And Scratch. That's the one who called you, the guy with the big eye."

"OK, so the bio teacher, the assistant principal, and the janitor are going to get us somehow?"

"You can laugh all you want, Zee. But sooner or later you're going to understand. You're going to believe."

"I'm trying to understand!" I was almost yelling now. "But this is all totally insane. You get that, right? This is not the way things are supposed to work."

"Yeah, I get it. And it's still the truth. They'll do anything to get what they want. There's a war coming, Zee. A battle to the death."

"A battle between a teenage heavy metal band and a high school janitor?"

"That's what it looks like on the outside. But on the inside, it's a lot bigger, a lot scarier, and way more important. And anyway, Scratch isn't really a janitor. He just was there yesterday to see you, to get at you. He won't be back with the mop and bucket. He'll take some other form."

"Like what? An evil librarian? The lunch lady from hell?"

"Making jokes won't change anything, Zee. What I'm saying is true. When the four true elements come together—fire and water, air and earth—then there's power like you can hardly imagine. Then it's real."

"What's real?"

"Think about it, Zee. What do gods have that mortals don't?"

"Funny names."

He scowled. "What else?" I thought of the Ghost Metal sound, the crowd at Waterstreet going nuts for us. "What else?" he demanded.

"You mean like people worshiping, making offerings?"

"And?"

"They live forever."

He nodded. "That's what Knacke wants. He's old, Zee. Way older than he looks. He's sick. And he's going to die soon if he doesn't get what he needs."

It was already way too much. Every answer he gave stirred up another dozen questions. My brain was already in overload mode. Words came out of Relly's mouth. And I guess I understood them. But it was too much. I started to shut down.

Soon enough he saw what was going on. "We should get on back," he said. "Are you cold?"

I nodded. He put his arm around me. It didn't drive off the cold. But the numb, faraway feeling wasn't so bad anymore.

Twelve

WE DID A NEW TUNE, with words from my notebook and music by Relly.

It was weirdly wild, full of sudden starts and stops, like a crash-test joy ride. I finally got the riff under my fingers and could whip it off just as fast as Relly. Of course, on the bass it was way heavier, like somebody tap-dancing with cement blocks strapped onto their feet.

"OK. I think we've got it down," Relly said after we'd run it a few times.

Jerod read over the lead sheet again, trying to figure out the words. "What does *hellebore* mean?"

"Ask Zee," Relly said.

"You wrote this?" He looked at me. I mean he really looked, eye to eye, for the first time.

"Yeah. Me and Relly together."

"So what does it mean?"

I felt like a slug, and Jerod was the guy with the salt.

In two seconds he'd pour the salt over me and I'd melt down to a nasty little puddle of goo.

"Well?"

"Hellebore is a poison plant. But in the olden days they used it to cure people who were crazy."

"It's a poison and it's a cure?"

"I don't know if it really works. Anyway, it sounded good and it fits in the song. And it rhymes with 'farthest shore.' "

"Yeah. I guess." It seemed like he really wanted to understand. My words and me too. He looked me over, from head to toe, like he'd never even noticed I was a girl before.

"It's no big deal," I said, getting more embarrassed by the minute. "If you don't like it, we'll change the words."

"No, no. It's OK. I don't care." Maybe he had really wanted to make sense of the song. But now it was too much work for him. So, with a shrug, he went back to being Cool Sneering Guy again.

He went to a way-better school than the rest of us, out in Pittsford with the other rich kids. He drove his dad's BMW. His dad was a big-deal lawyer and his mom wasn't a drunk like Butt's or gone off with a new husband and new family, like mine. He was headed to Cornell, like his father and his grandfather. Straight Ivy League. Upper crust. He let us know that whenever he could.

Relly had gone through three other singers before he

found Jerod. He was just what the band needed. Relly had that wispy, warlocky look. Butt was like a caveman. And I was me, invisible, behind and way down below. We needed somebody who looked great and loved to show off what he had.

So we put up with his whining and his rich-kid snottiness. And he put up with Relly's weirdness most of the time.

We did my new song, "The Rising Sigh," which was a phrase I got off a tombstone. Above the beautiful, terrible noise, Jerod poured out my words. I especially liked it when he closed his eyes and reached real high, like his brain was about to explode. I watched him from the side: his sleek shoulders, his gorgeous hair, the power in his arms as he clung to the mike stand, wailing.

Thirteen

I WAS SORT OF SLEEPING in English class, when there came a knocking on the door. I think we were supposed to be doing something with adverbs. Only, my worksheet was still untouched. I was floating in and out of dreamland, I guess, thinking about Mount Hope and Relly and the way his voice got real quiet and serious when he said, "Someday we'll be huge."

"Zee?" Mrs. Pelkey said. "Zee, you're wanted at the office by Mr. Franken."

I headed down to Frankengoon Central. I didn't even see who brought the note. Whoever it was had vanished by the time I got my stuff together. The halls were empty. It's always weird walking through a building that you know is full of people, but you can't see any of them. Voices behind closed doors, the whack-whack-whack of balls as I went by the gym, a nasty burning smell leaking out of Knacke's classroom.

I went to the main office. "Somebody said Mr. Franken wanted to see me." The lady behind the desk looked over her glasses, scowling like I was a wriggling little bug. Her lipstick was bright red and kind of smeared. There was a bluish wart on the side of her nose. She didn't even speak, just pointed with her well-chewed pencil to the open door.

So I went in and Frankengoon told me to have a seat. He was a huge man, way over six foot tall. He stooped a little, like it was hard to keep all that chest and shoulders and bulging head upright.

"You're not doing well in your academics, Zee. You know that, correct?" His voice sounded like it came from a deep black hole in the ground. "Your grades have been slipping steadily this year. And now I have heard some very disturbing reports from Mr. Knacke."

There was no point in me denying it. Whatever he said, whatever lies Knacke made up, Frankengoon would believe them. Did he claim I was selling drugs in class? Making out with some guy in the back of the library? Coming to school with Cream Ale on my breath?

No, those were too normal. Knacke would accuse me of something totally bizarro.

"I have a report from Mr. Knacke, and I have physical evidence, that you have been engaged in—" He was struggling to find the right words. "You have been taking part in certain rituals, certain occult practices, which we cannot allow to continue on school property. Indeed, if Mr. Knacke is correct, you may be breaking the law too." He leaned in close and it was like a massive stone monument was bending down toward me. "I can't emphasize this enough, Zee. You are going down a path which will only lead to great suffering, to disaster." His huge breath wheezed in and out.

I had no idea what he was talking about. "Evidence?" I asked. It was all so stupid, so wrong.

"Yes, evidence." He opened a desk drawer and pulled out a clear plastic bag. Inside was a notebook. Yeah, it was mine. And yeah, I thought I'd lost it the day before. Now I knew where it had gone.

"This is yours, correct?" He didn't wait for an answer. "Mr. Knacke found this in class recently and he thought it important that I know about its existence."

Carefully, he opened the bag and slid the notebook out. "The words you've written here, Zee, are very disturbing. If I didn't know better, I would say they are the product of a diseased mind."

I grabbed for it, trying to get it away from him. But he just stood up, and the notebook was way out of reach.

"What you've written here, and drawn here, is very troubling."

"They're just lyrics to songs. That's all." And some

sketches I made. Relly's hands on the Strat's neck. They were small, and yet they were strong too. Totally sure of what they were doing, his fingers reached to make a chord that had no name.

Frankengoon just stared at me with those huge yellowy eyes.

"I'm in a band, OK?" I said. "There's no law against that. Those are just lyrics to songs me and Relly wrote. It's no big deal."

"No big deal?" He was almost yelling now. "These words are very disturbing, Zee. Vile, occult ravings. You're allowing your mind to travel a truly dangerous path."

He thumbed through the book, and I had the same sick feeling as if he was peeking at me through the bathroom window. "Give it back!" I pleaded.

He shook his head. "What does this mean? 'Beautiful City of the Dead.'"

"It's just a song. That's what they used to call Mount Hope in the olden days."

He turned a few pages. "And this?" His voice was shaking, like he was about to explode.

"We see our friends are round us falling.
We see them buried deep in dust.
In solemn silence yet they're calling.
Prepare for death, for die you must."

"It's the poem off a gravestone. I didn't even make it up." I could feel the tears coming. These were precious words, private words, and he was sneering at them out loud like they were dirty sayings scrawled on a desktop.

Somebody had carved these words on the stones and it was like a voice from two hundred years back talking directly to me.

"Give it back, please?" The worst thing was me having to beg to get back the notebook. "There's nothing bad there. It's beautiful, not wrong."

He glared down at me. "Do you know what happens to young people who get deeply involved in the occult?"

"It's not occult!" I whispered. "It's just words on gravestones."

"Mr. Knacke is convinced that a secret occult conclave has worked its way into the student body here. He, and I, are determined that this school will not be a breeding ground for evil." He said *evil* like it was poison he had to get out of his mouth.

"You've been warned, Zee. We will not tolerate occult practices here. We will do all we must to protect the student body. You can go now."

"I want my notebook back," I said as I got up.

"Out of the question."

"It's mine! I didn't do anything wrong. Give it back!"

"I am keeping this in a safe place. If the time comes that I must use it as evidence against you, Zee, I certainly will. Consider yourself lucky that I have not already contacted the police in this matter."

He loomed toward me, like a dragon rising up from its lair. No flames spewed from his mouth, but I wouldn't have been surprised if they had.

Fourteen

"I JUST WANT PEOPLE to leave me alone," I said. "That's all. I'm not fighting anyone. Anyway, they already won. There's no point fighting."

"So you're quitting before you even start?" Relly said.

"I don't want to be a god." This sounded stupid, but it was true. "I don't want to be in your secret war and fight against Knacke and Scratch."

"All right," Relly said. "What do you want?" We were in the kitchen. His mom was mixing up herbs to make one of her stinky teas. She kept looking over at me, then back to the leaves and roots and berries she was crushing up.

"I want to be in the band. And play out. And maybe do some recording."

"That's it? If you could have anything in the whole world, that's the best you can come up with?"

Tannis stared at me, like she was afraid of what I'd say.

Or maybe she was holding her words inside until the right moment to speak.

"I don't know," I whispered. "What difference does it make? I can't have what I want."

"Who says?"

If I was completely honest, I would have told him, "I want you. You're the one I've been waiting for."

But I couldn't say that with his mom in the room with us. And maybe I couldn't say it even if we were totally alone. I wasn't afraid he'd laugh or make a disgusted face. No, much worse would be a shrug and him saying, "Yeah, sure, whatever."

"OK, maybe you're right and it doesn't matter what you want," Relly told me after a while. "Then the only thing that counts is what you are." He took my hands and held them, which he'd never done before. It felt wonderful and scary, perfectly natural and totally wrong. "You're a god, Zee, like me. Like Butt and Jerod. And gods have got to—"

"Butt and Jerod? They burst into flame, too?"

"No, that's just me. They're made of different stuff. Butt is earth. And Jerod is air. I'm fire, which you already know."

"And that makes me—"

Tannis cut in. "Water." Her voice was loud and edgy. "Your element is water, Zee." She was holding a glass mixing bowl. The stuff inside sloshed back and forth like liquid silver. She came toward me and for a second, I thought she was going to pour it over my head. Instead, she set it carefully on the table. "Look," she said. And there was a reflection of my face on the surface. It flickered and shook. But still I saw myself.

"You're water," Relly said. "And that makes Scorpio Bone complete. Earth, air, water, and fire. The four elements."

"So Knacke is right? You're into—"

"Knacke is a stenching old scumpack and everything he touches turns rotten."

He continued to hold my hands in his. And they were strong, real strong. "You know what the word *occult* really means, Zee?" Of course I didn't. "All it means is 'secret' or 'hidden.' It doesn't have a thing to do with good or bad. Just secret."

"And Scorpio Bone is the—"

"Four and no more. It takes four to win the war." Relly was looking at me eye to eye and it was the total opposite of when Frankengoon had stared me down. Both times, somebody was peering deep into me. But with Relly it felt good, like he knew me, maybe even knew me better than I knew myself. And I was not just OK, but great, the one and only. There was something about me that was precious and powerful. And Relly needed it. He needed me.

"There's four of us, two pairs. Butt is earth. You know:

all his stupid toilet jokes. He's the god of dirt. And Jerod's his opposite, the god of the air. Singers are all wind, right? Blowing hard, but kind of empty. Jerod and Butt are one pair. The lowly dirt and the heavenly air."

"And we're the other pair?"

He nodded. "Fire and water. You need me to bring you to a boil. And I need you to put out the flames. But you're not just plain water. You're ice and you're snow. You're steam and clouds and fog."

"And fever," Tannis said. "Fever is body heat cooking the body's water. Fire and water together in the flesh." Saying this, she went back to the stove.

"This is all so insane. I just want to—"

"Don't say it unless you really and truly know what you want. Because you might just get it."

"All right. So what do *you* want?" I asked him.

His mom turned to watch Relly. He didn't see the look on her face. But I did. And it was scarier than anything Frankengoon or even Knacke had done. It was like the answer to my question was life or death to her. The wrong response and everything would be ruined.

"I want the band to be a success. I want to play out a lot, too, and record. And I want people to see how great we are."

"But that's not all?"

"I guess I want the real thing," he said after a long

stretch of quiet. "I mean, if it's fake or bogus I hate it. If it's all lies, then I want nothing to do with it. TV and text-books and what kids talk about at school. That's all a lie. You know what I mean?"

He could see I didn't understand.

"Like you look at me and I'm just this kid. But I'm also the god of fire. And you're just a kid too, a girl with an Ibanez bass who doesn't say hardly anything at school. And you're the ocean too, and rain, and blizzards."

Part of me was saying, *Right, sure, I'm Neptuna, goddess of the seas,* and thinking about how crazy it all sounded. I should go home and never come back. Next thing I knew, he'd be talking about human sacrifice or having aliens over for supper.

But another part was listening real hard and kind of nodding. It was like I knew it all already, only I needed somebody to bring the truth back to mind.

"You really believe this, don't you? The god part. Earth, wind, fire, and water. The whole bit. You believe it?"

"One hundred percent." He didn't pause for even a second to answer that one.

His mom turned away, back to messing around with her wet leaves and lumps of little black berries.

I let out all the air I'd been holding in my chest. I closed my eyes and relaxed. "All right, then," I said. "Then I believe it, too."

Fifteen

THAT NIGHT, SCRATCH ATTACKED. I don't mean he kicked the front door down and burst in swinging. Or came crawling out of the phone like a snaky ghost. No, it was-n't broken windows or bloody threats. All the same, it was an attack. And it made me even more a believer in what Relly had said that day.

As usual, the house was empty when I got home. My dad was out, at work, I guess. And I had no idea when he'd be back. I nuked some four-cheese lasagna and ate it standing at the kitchen sink. It was good, real good. My dad's cooking was always the best. And he always made sure there was something excellent waiting for me in the fridge.

I could see a faint reflection of my face in the kitchen window. Only, for a minute it didn't really look like me. I stopped eating, put my plate in the sink, and stared. Who was it, if not me? Was I getting so crazy that I didn't even know my own face? Slowly, the little jab of panic faded. Yeah, that was me, I told myself, not some stalker peering in.

After checking a third time to make sure all the doors were locked, I went upstairs.

I kept hearing weird noises. Usually the scratching of tree limbs on the windows didn't bug me at all. Usually I was fine with the house creaking softly, like the distant noise of my dad's bedsprings as he settled in for sleep. Most times, the hum of the furnace was a comfort when I was alone.

That night, however, everything seemed wrong.

There was still mist on the bathroom mirror, though nobody had used the tub all day. The numbers on my alarm clock were flashing, like when the power has gone off. Only, they weren't pulsing in a regular beat. They flashed quickly, then were steady, then throbbed and faded and came back twice as bright.

The worst thing, though, was when I opened my bass case and took out my Ibanez. I wrapped my fingers around the neck and knew somebody had been playing it, somebody with grimy hands.

Now, I'm very careful about wiping it down after I play. I have special rags to rub the strings and I make sure the neck is dry before I put the bass away.

So the feel of the neck, kind of cold and sticky, scared me as much as it grossed me out. Somebody had been looking through my stuff, messing around with it, leaving a faint trail of black fingerprints. And that somebody, I knew, was Scratch.

I guess I could've run. But I didn't know where my dad was at that hour. And I didn't think Relly's mom would be too thrilled to find me back there, banging on her door. I thought about Butt. I knew he'd be fine with me showing up at his place. Only I'd never been there and didn't know if I could find it at night.

Call the police? Right, they'd love to hear some kid blabbering about steam on the bathroom mirror and ick on her bass.

So what I did surprised even me. I called information and asked for the number of Festus B. Knacke.

"Yes? Hello?" He sounded different than at school, older, a lot older. I wondered if he dyed his hair, wore dentures, maybe even some kind of corset to school to pull in his gut and make him stand up straighter. "What is it?"

I was quiet for a minute. A couple times, back in middle school, I'd done some phone pranks. This was different. I wasn't silent to bug Knacke. No, I was afraid, and I was full of doubt.

"Is anyone there?" he asked. "Hello?"

"Uh, yeah, this is Zee. You know, from sixth-period bio."

"Yes?"

"I, uh, I'm calling to tell you—"

He was listening, close. He waited.

"Scratch was here, in my house. I don't know how he got in. But he was here."

No response.

"Well, I'm just calling to say that we've got you figured out. Me and Relly. We know all about you. Frankengoon had me dragged down to the office today and he showed me the notebook you stole. It's mine and you've got no right taking it. I want it back."

"What you want and what you can have are two different—"

"You can't just steal my stuff! It's private. It's got nothing to do with school. I wasn't causing any trouble. It's mine and you've got to give it back."

"I think it would be best if we continued this discussion tomorrow. Speaking face to face is always better, don't you agree?" Now his voice was oily as a talk show host's. He was back in charge. I yelled and made demands. He was smooth and in control now. "We'll discuss this at school. I'll make sure that Mr. Franken can join us."

"I don't want—"

"Goodnight, Zee," he said, and hung up.

Sixteen

OK, SO I'M A GOD and I can't even get my notebook back from an old man with bad breath.

Relly had said I was water—rushing streams, snow, ice, and fog. So then why couldn't I just pound Knacke with a blizzard? I even tried it, sort of. I went to the window and reached out my hands and made some magic gestures like I'd seen in the movies. I pictured a huge black cloud swirling down from the night sky and blasting Knacke to his knees.

Of course, nothing happened. He was probably asleep and snoring like a great nasty bug. Buzz, gasp, buzz.

I ran the faucet in the bathroom. I concentrated and tried to make the water rise up and do my will. It just flowed out in a steady stream and went down the drain.

Then I went downstairs and turned on the teakettle. When the water was boiling, I looked closely at the jet of steam. It whistled like it always did. I put my hand into the steam for just a second. And it hurt, like I knew it would.

Right, I'm a god. I have secret powers. I looked at the dishes in the sink. Maybe that was it. Maybe I was Super Dishwasher Girl.

I didn't bother trying my amazing powers on the lasagna pan.

Seventeen

SCHOOL WAS OK THE next day. Classes went by in a boring blur. Lunch was fairly disgusting, as it always was. And my favorite drummer made his usual butt jokes. He seemed to think that a "feces statement" was a lot better to include in his essay than a "thesis statement."

"Get it? Get it? Feces statement!"

"Right, I got it."

Happy now, he wiggled a couple of strands of spaghetti over his gaping mouth and made monster noises.

Then there was bio. I thought about skipping. I was ready to do it. But Relly was hanging around by my locker before class and said I had to be there.

"Why? So Knacke can wave my notebook around and tell everyone I'm a cult leader? Yeah, that sounds like a lot of fun. Maybe he'll want to burn me at the stake like a Salem witch. I can hardly wait."

"The witches there weren't burned. They were all hanged."

"Enough, all right? I was just making a joke. I don't care about the Salem witch trials."

"Well, you'd better be in class."

So I went.

Knacke was all excited about his new fungus. He'd brought in a big hunk of rotten wood and as soon as we all settled down, he turned out the lights. He'd already drawn the blinds and taped heavy paper over the windows. As our eyes got used to the darkness, we all saw what he was so thrilled about.

A faint greenish glow was coming from the fungus. Knacke didn't talk for a while. He let us stare at the broken tree stump. Some kids were impressed. Some asked questions but he hushed them. Some wanted to come up to the front and look closer. This he was OK with.

So row by row went and got up close and personal with a hunk of glowing rotten wood.

When it was my turn, I kind of hung back. "Come on, come on, Zee," Knacke said, smiling. "This is a wonderful chance to—"

Blah blah blah. I wasn't listening. I was looking over at the Smoking Man, who sat in the corner. His face was greenish now, like he was sick from all that nicotine and tar.

I guess Knacke explained about how the fungus created

its own light. And he told us about some fish and slime molds that did it too. I wasn't paying attention. Any minute, I kept thinking, he's going to go off on me, yelling about my notebook and the so-called occult crowd I was hanging around with.

Only that day it never came. He was so caught up in his glowing clump of wood that I guess he forgot about me and the phone call.

He opened the door and the light from the hallway flooded in. Squinting against it, I followed the rest of the kids out. No sneers, no nasty comments, no threats from Knacke.

And that made it worse. Passing by Knacke, I was sure this was just the calm before the thunderstorm, the smooth seas before the tidal wave hits and tears the boat to shreds.

Eighteen

"I'M GOING, WITH OR without you," I told Relly.

"It's breaking and entering," he said. "It's against the law, you know. If you get caught—"

"I'm getting into school tonight and I'm getting my notebook back. Are you in or out?"

He didn't hesitate. "I'm in. But we got to make it perfect. We can't screw up, all right?"

All through practice that night, I kept looking at Jerod and wondering what it meant that he was the god of air. Yeah, he was the singer. Only, there had to be more to it. For all his big talk and stuck-up ways, he really was a lightweight, wispy as the wind. Way more than the rest of us, Jerod acted most like a god should. Full of himself, proud and self-assured. And he looked like one too. But when it came down to it, he was just too into himself for this kind of thing. Making the band a success—definitely. Helping Zee out—forget it.

So I didn't want him along when we broke into school.

And I watched Butt too, while we ran through our set list.

When he was bored, Butt would squeeze his hand under his armpit to make blapping noises or try to crush a Jolt can against his forehead. He was like a big toddler kid. Six feet tall and still he acted like a two year old sometimes. I think he went right from his baby rattle to a drum set. He wasn't stupid. That's not what I mean. He was simple. Which is different than being a feeb. He liked a couple of things and that was all he needed.

Big-metal noise. Butt jokes. Working on his van. Pizza and wings. Girls, but only to look at, not to talk to. He wasn't quite ready for that.

I liked Butt, and I trusted him. When we needed muscles, raw pigheaded power, he was the one.

Tonight, however, I figured we needed stealth and cool wits. So it was just me and Relly who went off after practice to reclaim my notebook.

I'd already taken care of getting past the alarm system. I managed to get some detention in English, and I knew I could unlatch one of the windows when Mrs. Pelkey wasn't looking. So unless the janitor checked every sensor in the building, we had an easy entry.

So far so good. We put some cement blocks by the

window, climbed up, and were through. No sirens, no flashing lights.

It was very weird to be there so late. Everything was familiar and foreign at the same time. Yeah, those were desks, only they looked like the shadowy wreckage of a lost jungle city. Over there was the blackboard, still with names and dates in Mrs. Pelkey's scrawl. Now, however, the writing was pure gibberish, forgotten tomb paintings.

We tiptoed through the classroom and into the hallway. Way at the end, a red exit light was throbbing. The rows of steel lockers and the shiny, bare floor made it seem like we'd broken into an ancient underground chamber. OK, I told myself, you're a god and maybe this is your temple.

"Which way?" Relly whispered.

I pointed and we went toward Frankengoon's office.

The darkness was strange, but much stranger was the silence there. I say "silence," because I don't have any other word for it. It seemed to breathe, to pulse slowly in and out as though the whole building was alive.

We got to the main office and found that the door was locked.

"OK, now what?" Relly asked. I was in charge. Success or failure, it was all up to me.

"Here goes nothing." I took a set of keys out of my pocket. I'd paid fifty dollars for them, to a kid named Marky Blood. For a price, he could provide just about anything. Mostly that meant pot and vodka and Trojans. But he dealt in other things too.

"Well, let's see if Marky's made a fool of me," I said.

The key slid in smoothly, like a hot knife into butter. It turned just as smoothly and the door came open without a sound.

"All right," I said. "We're in."

We went straight through the main office and into Frankengoon's inner chamber. I'd seen him take my notebook from his desk. However, searching every drawer, I came up with nothing. Something like panic, but softer, more blurred and oozy, was pouring into my body. "He was standing right here with it."

"We can't search the whole school," Relly said.

I gave a quick scan to the bookshelves and the cabinet full of old football trophies. "I can't believe it. We came all this way—"

And then we heard the footsteps.

I just about threw up right there, the fear was so strong. And seeing the look on Relly's face didn't help. The sound was slow and shuffling, like an old man. "Maybe it's a night watchman," I whispered. "We can hide here and wait till he's gone."

Then I saw my notebook. Frankengoon had wrapped it in a half dozen plastic bags, like it was infected with the most deadly virus in the world. There the notebook was, square on top of his desk. In the weird light, all bound up in plastic, it looked like a slab of rock flaked off a meteor.

I grabbed it, clutched it to my chest. Relly took me by the arm and hissed, "Let's go."

We made it to the corridor. But then we saw him: Smoking Man come to life.

He had his cowboy hat on, and three cigarettes hung from his mouth, burning. He had one in each hand too. And as he shuffled toward us the smoke curled and churned around him.

I just about lost it. I mean, the surge of panic came up strong and just about washed away every thought in my head. I clung to my notebook and stared.

He was a dummy, just plastic. And yet he was alive. The little pump that made his fake lungs work was wheezing in and out. His feet didn't leave the floor, but dragged along the shiny tiles. He looked at us, and beneath the brim of his cowboy hat two red coals burned where his eyes should have been.

With one great rattling intake, he sucked smoke into himself. And with one hollow groan he jetted the filthy cloud at me.

"Give," he said, reaching for the notebook.

I shook my head, as if arguing with a zombie cowboy made any sense.

"Give," he repeated. It was Scratch's voice, low and gritty.

Holding the notebook hard against my chest was exactly the right thing to do. It kept me from losing my supper. It seemed to hold me up straight. And the words, the inscriptions from the graveyard, somehow passed through the plastic and into my body.

A law eternal does decree
that all things born should mortal be.

Smoking Man had us trapped. We had to get past him to escape. And his stinking cloud made a kind of barrier too.

I was pretty useless now. I mean, I wasn't screaming in hysterics. But I was paralyzed, staring at Smoking Man's plastic corpse face.

It was Relly who got us out of there.

He was fire. And he was strong when it counted. Relly came across as kind of flimsy and frail. But when he had to, onstage in front of a thousand kids or now up against Smoking Man, he didn't back down.

He was a god of fire, and figured that was exactly what it would take to defeat Smoking Man. So he lunged at him, threw himself at the shuffling cowboy. And his hands caught fire, I'm sure of it, as soon as he grappled with Smoking Man. They kind of wrestled there in slow motion, bitter billows swirling around them. Relly cursed as he fought with burning hands. Smoking Man groaned. I clutched my notebook and thought of rain.

This might seem strange. But that's what filled my head as I watched Smoking Man pushing Relly to the floor. My friend, my only real friend, was being strangled by a filthy plastic dummy and I thought of rain.

Relly's fires were snuffed out. His voice, too. Smoking Man had him by the neck, squeezing.

And then the sprinkler right over them burst and poured down a steady stream.

I watched the water fall, a silvery jet from above. I focused everything on that wet, saving blast. The fire sprinklers are supposed to come on in zones. A whole wing or hallway is supposed to get drenched if any of them come on. That night it was just one, right above Relly and our enemy.

In a minute it was over. Smoking Man lay broken and lifeless, black mud running out of his mouth. Relly pulled out from under him and grabbed my hand. "Let's go, let's go!" he hissed.

And we went, out the open window and across the wet grass of the soccer field.

Nineteen

THE NEXT NIGHT, we were eating pizza, the four of us around Relly's kitchen table. Real greasy and gooey and still bubbling hot. And as usual, I bit into a slice without waiting and burned a blister on the roof of my mouth. But I guess I didn't care that night because I kept on eating and burning myself, shoveling the pizza in.

We had a couple of quarts of Relly's Panther Blood that he got from the old Italian market. You know, a place with bulging yellow cheeses hanging down and Frank Sinatra crooning in the background and guys with big hairy arms cutting meat in back. They had drinks from Italy too, and this stuff was Relly's fave. It had some fancy Italian name nobody could pronounce. So we went with what Relly called it: Panther Blood.

It tasted kind of like Pepsi. Only there was something bitter mixed in too, like orange rind and cinnamon and cloves. At first I hated the stuff. It was purplish brown and had a little fizz to it. I'd sniffed it and put it aside. "Go on. It won't hurt you," Relly'd said. "Matter of fact, it's better than Mountain Dew and Jolt mixed together. Puts a shine on everything."

Relly was all cranked up, excited about defeating Smoking Man and about our next gig too, opening up for Kruel and Unusual at the Bug Jar. "It's all coming together," he said. "We're strong and we're getting stronger all the time."

He had another slug of the Panther Blood. "Putting together a band is alchemy," he went on. "Like making a secret formula. You got to have all the right elements and you mix them together under exactly the right conditions."

Jerod just wanted to hear about the gig. Money, we were going to get paid real money to play. And we'd be on the bill with a real band from out of town. Kruel and Unusual even had a CD that got some college radio play. We were heading for the Big Time, and heading there fast.

Twenty

THE GOOD LUCK JUST kept coming. Knacke was out sick again, and the sub didn't make us do any work. Smoking Man didn't reappear in the classroom. Nobody got dragged down to the office and grilled about the wreckage we'd left in the hall. I guess the janitor had found the burned-up dummy the next day and tossed him in the dumpster.

And almost as good, both Jerod and Butt got their own wheels that week.

Jerod had been driving his dad's BMW. But for his birthday he got his own car, a brand-new Acura.

Butt took the driver's test again and finally passed. So now he could actually drive the beat-up van he'd been working on since he was twelve. It was a heap, held together with bungee cords and duct tape. Still, it ran. And he was happy to give me and Relly rides in the Buttmobile whenever he could.

I even felt healthy, for the first time that school year. A whole week with no runny nose. No more fevers. No more heavy pressure in my chest, like someone was standing on me and squeezing out all my breath.

And with the notebook back, it was like I'd reclaimed some part of myself. There were my first versions of the Scorpio Bone logo. There was the page where I'd written Relly's name about a hundred times. I wasn't even embarrassed now to see it. Most important, there were all the lyrics for our songs. Some were mine, and some were copied straight from stones in Mount Hope.

It bothered me a little, to think that Knacke and Frankengoon had been poking around in the notebook. Still, I had it back. It was all there, unharmed.

I sat with Relly in his attic, reading through the poetry, enjoying again the creaky rhymes and strange images. Who were these people, I wondered, who had such words of doom carved above their heads? I mean, I had names and dates for them, but still they seemed as alien as if they'd come from another planet.

> *Though worms my poor body*
> *may claim as their prey,*
> *'Twill outshine when rising*
> *the sun at midday.*

Again and again the poems talked about "rising." At the end of the world, I guessed, these people thought they'd come up from the ground. But not as crumbling, poxy old bones. No, I pictured them as pure light, beautiful, shining, happy. It wasn't all doom and gloom. No, there was real hope there on some of the stones. Hope and a weird kind of joy.

"Hey, what do you think about this one?" I asked Relly.

Be wise ye living while you may
Prepare against the coming day
When you as low as I must lay
Your souls from hence be called away.

We'd been back to Mount Hope and collected more inscriptions. I had this idea that some day we'd cut an entire CD with songs based on the gravestone writings.

"You think this one is about going to heaven? 'Your souls from hence be called away.' " I read aloud.

"Maybe."

"Maybe what?"

"Maybe heaven or maybe right here on earth. Didn't you ever know anyone who heard a call? It's mostly people who go to church. But not always."

"So you did? You heard a call?" I asked.

He pointed to his Strat in its half-opened case. The finish was beautiful amber red. The strings shone like silver veins. "Sure. I heard it loud and clear. The monster riff, the Ghost Metal noise. Spirits screaming through the amps."

When he talked this way, I felt myself falling, like I was out in the ocean and forgot how to swim. I was going down, down, down. Soon enough the waves would close over my head and I'd be lost forever.

I read girl magazines sometimes, though I didn't want anyone to know it. Makeup tips, dating, weight loss, workout routines. I tried to find somebody in those slick pages who was like me. I tried to find something I might care about, and then maybe I'd be a tiny bit normal. It embarrassed me, actually. Why should I care? I had Scorpio Bone. I had Relly and my Ibanez and my notebook full of weird old sayings. Why should I care about such trivial stuff as boyfriends and new fashions?

But I even thought of writing to an advice column.

"I have this problem. I'm the only girl in a band. And we're gods too. We have secret powers. Water and fire and air and earth. And there's these old creepy guys who want to destroy us. Only I'm not sure why. My main problem is knowing if the lead guitarist loves me or if he just likes the way I play bass. He also bursts into flames sometimes. So what should I do? Play it cool like I don't care, or be myself and let him know what I feel? Any advice would be a big help. Thanks."

Yeah, they print a lot of letters like that. Right in with the four-page spreads on new mascara shades, there's usually an article about teenage heavy metal gods and the evil forces they face.

Twenty-one

OUR NEXT HOT DATE was on the Broad Street bridge. This is where you can get the best view of the Genesee. I know our river isn't the Nile or the Amazon, but for me it has a power. Especially seen from the bridge. The gorge walls are cold raw stone. Old brick buildings crowd along the upper banks. The water is gray and fierce and forever.

Looking across the river, Relly pointed out to me the great statue of Hermes that jutted against the winter sky. The ancient copper god was way up there, on top of a stone spire, reaching heavenward, running due north like the river itself. "Over twenty feet tall," Relly said. It had been there, off and on, for over a hundred years. First, looming above some factory in the way-olden days. In the early '50s it got taken down when they did urban renewal. Later on, it was retrieved from its storage place and lifted back up to stand guard over the city, the river, the bridge.

Relly knew all about it. He did research at the library,

which was just across the river, in plain sight of Hermes. He'd spent time in the local-history room, digging through old files of newspaper clippings. "They keep calling him Mercury in the paper," Relly said. "But the real name is Hermes."

"They brought him back in November of 1974. Think about it. Zeppelin was ruling the universe then. Black Sabbath, too, Judas Priest and Blue Oyster Cult, all the old metal gods. They brought him down from the sky and fastened him there at the top of that tower. He weighs seven hundred pounds. That's heavy metal."

Beneath us flowed the river, full of clotted ice and logs stripped bare of their bark, wreckage from a hundred miles upstream. "X marks the spot," Relly said. "This was where the canal once went. Did you know that? The Erie Canal ran right here. It flowed over an aqueduct, east-west canal crossing the north-south river. And who should be reigning, watching, standing above that place but Hermes himself."

Yeah, it was all pseudomystical crot from the pit of Relly's brain. I mean, the facts were right. But what he made out of them was his typical bizarro story.

"This is the place," he said. Calm, matter of fact. "Right here. This is your place, Zee. Where the canal crosses the river. And Hermes reigns above." His voice changed, like he was reading from some old book of spells. "Where the ghost of water crosses the north-flowing stream and the Winged God stands supreme."

I ignored the mystical stuff, at least for a little while. "The canal went right here?" I asked.

"Yeah. They just added another layer to the aqueduct when they turned it into a bridge. If you look from the Court Street bridge"—which was the next one upriver—"you can see it's different. Layers of stone, different layers of time."

We looked toward the library, which was built on the edge of the river. Water poured out from underneath, into the gorge. Eleven arched spillways. "The river goes right below. There's places in the basement of the library where you can lift up these manhole covers and there's the river, black and secret."

Water, water, water. Lost canals over rivers that ran under buildings. Hidden streams. Falls and rapids.

"This is the place, Zee. Here's where it will all come to an end."

Twenty-two

AN OLD HOMELESS GUY was heading toward us, looking over the edge of the bridge as he shambled along. He had about a dozen grocery bags all bulging and ripped. His shoes were patched with duct tape. He was hunched over. And he smelled bad. Even from a distance, I caught a whiff.

"Maybe we should get going," I said.

"Crot Almighty," Relly hissed. "It's happening already."

"What?"

Then I saw who the old guy was: Scratch.

He turned his big saggy left eye toward me. And he grinned.

"I didn't think," Relly said, "it would be so soon." He was afraid. That was obvious. He turned and looked behind, as if expecting Knacke and Frankengoon to be coming at us.

But it was just Scratch that day.

He came up close but didn't seem to notice Relly at

first. He talked to me, just me. His voice was familiar, gritty and hoarse. "I thought you'd be here." He looked over the edge of the bridge, into the churning gray flood. "You found your element. You know who you are now, right? Where water crosses water."

"Let's go," I hissed, clutching at Relly's coat sleeve.

"What's your hurry?" Scratch said. "You found the place. *Your* place."

Now it was Relly who clutched at me. "Don't listen to him. Don't pay any—"

"I'm just here to make an offer," Scratch said. "If you got something better, sonny boy, I'm sure she'll take you up on it." He smiled with his filthy, rotting teeth.

"You're water, Zee. And we need water. Mr. Franken is air. Mr. Knacke is fire. As you can see, I'm earth. We've lost our water. She's gone. Gone for good. Gone, gone, gone. We need you, Zee. And we have a thousand times more to offer than your little teenage pip-squeak friends."

He dropped his bags and stood up straight. He opened up his ratty old bum's coat and thumped his fist on his heart. Puffs of black dust rose up, making a filthy halo around his head. "Our power is ancient. Deep. And forever. Your little kiddy friends will dry up and blow away like leaves. We'll still be here. We are eternal. You can be part of that, Zee."

On the other side of the bridge, people were walking.

Cars passed. A short distance away, a businessman was feeding quarters into his parking meter. And there they were, a fire god and an earth god fighting over the water.

A ripple of blue flame ran down Relly's left arm and burst off his fingers. Scratch caught it and snuffed it out as you might catch a bit of fluff floating in the air. He sneered at Relly. "That's all you've got, kid? Little tricks like that?"

Relly spat a wad of blue flame. It hit Scratch in the chest and died. Scratch laughed and I swear I could smell graveyard dirt on his breath.

I thought they were going to go at it just as they had when Scratch was inside Smoking Man. Two guys fighting. Young versus old. Fiery fists and living human dirt.

"Stop it!" I snarled at them both. "No more. Understand?"

"Fine, fine," Scratch said. "I'm just here to pass along the offer. Join us, Zee. Dump these pimple-faced losers and join up with us. You'll never regret it. Four and no more, as it was before." He smiled his rotted smile. "And shall be forever."

With that, he gave me a wink, like we'd already made some secret deal. He turned and shuffled back the way he'd come. We watched him for a long while. Across the bridge, down the street, and then lost in the crowd.

Twenty-three

PRACTICE THAT NIGHT WAS strange. We sounded good, maybe better than ever. Still, Relly's attic felt like a tomb. It was colder than it ever had been. The sounds of Scorpio Bone banged around in the high reaches of the roof like a swarm of bats. The bare light bulbs hanging down flickered, almost dying a few times. And the amps cut in and out too, as though our power was being stolen, enemy hands grabbing at the wires far away.

We did a new song. It had no words yet, just three chords and a jagged Orion Hedd kind of riff. I kept thinking, *Here's our power, here's something they'll never have. Why would I join up with disgusting old men when I can make this awesome, fearsome noise?*

We kept going over and over the song, till Jerod complained. "Maybe you guys can do this after I go? How 'bout something where I actually sing?"

We agreed. And when he drove home to Pittsford in

his Acura, we came back to the tune.

"So what are we going to call it?" Relly asked. He looked to me for the words now. I had taken over that job in the band.

"How about a person's name? Like this was their theme song?" I asked.

I collected names too, not just gravestone poetry. I mean, spending my whole life explaining about "Zee," the olden-day names from the graveyard made me feel almost normal.

There were the Greek and Roman names in Mount Hope: Socrates Good, Electra Wheeler, Parthenon Bradford, Livi Lee, and Julius Jones.

There were a few of the old Puritan names too. These were much stranger. Fearing Swift, Resolved Stevens, Pardon Davies, Thankful Pratt, Return Wilson. "How about 'Silence Loud?' " I said. That was my favorite. After seeing her stone, I kept thinking what it would be like to go around my whole life with a name like that.

"Silence Loud. Perfect," Relly said.

"Silence Loud," Butt repeated, slamming the kick drum and setting us off again.

Twenty-four

"THIS IS HOW IT WORKS. There's not just us, I mean Scorpio Bone. There's other tetrads. Dozens, maybe hundreds. Four and no more. All the world o'er. From then and always, till the end of days."

Tetrads was the word for us. For Knacke's Krew. And I guess for other groups of four, hidden away in plain sight everywhere.

"Led Zeppelin. Totally. No question about it," Relly said. "The Fantastic Four, of course. Black Sabbath and Slayer. And I think there were four Gospels in the Bible. Matthew, Mark, Luke, and John. Right? There's other people out there like us. They need each other. Earth, Wind, Air, and Fire. They need the full tetrad to be complete. You know what I mean?"

"Sort of." We were walking across the Platt Street bridge. It was closed off to cars years ago. Now only people can go across, and look down into the deepest part of the river gorge. This late in the year, there wasn't much water coming down the high falls. Still, it was a pretty amazing place. Round and deep, with crumbling rock walls, it was bigger than a stadium. And it was right in the middle of the city, a vast secret hole.

"Some people say that when you fall in love, it's like finding a piece of yourself you never knew was missing. Well this is way better." Relly was holding my hand. We looked down into the gorge together. "We're not like regular people. It takes four for us."

"Four and no more," I murmured.

"That's right. We found our four and we're going straight to the top. That's why Knacke is so obsessed with you. He needs a fourth to make his tetrad complete again."

"So what happened to her?"

Relly shrugged.

"It was a her, right? A girl?"

"My mom says it's a guy thing to obsess about fire. You know how little boys are so nuts about candles and matches? A four-year-old kid will do anything so he can play with a campfire, right? Get a burning stick going and wave it around. My mom says you don't learn that. You're born with it."

"I get that. I read that almost all pyros are guys. But what about Knacke's lost fourth? Was that a girl?"

"Yeah."

We were leaning over the guardrail, looking into the abyss. The logical part of my brain said we were safe. They made these fences strong enough and high enough to keep people from going over. But another part of me was scream-ing like a siren, telling me I would die if I didn't get away from there fast.

Relly dropped a stone and we watched it fall—the whole way down. When it hit the water, the splash was too small to see.

"My mom says it's normal to think about doing it. Not healthy, just normal. Everyone thinks about jumping in some time."

This made me even more afraid. Had he been reading my mind?

"What are you talking about?" I said.

"There's some impulse—that's what she calls it—an impulse to do it—to throw yourself in. 'We all want to return to our element.' That's what she says."

"So what happened to her?"

"My mom?"

"No, whoever it was that used to be Knacke's fourth."

"We all go back to our element. Some sooner. Some later."

We watched the silvery chain of the high falls a long time. The water came and fell and ran away. But it never ran out. It never stopped.

"Maybe that's what Knacke is so afraid of now. Why he's acting so weird. Maybe he thinks he's got to burn up—go back to his element—now that the tetrad is missing a piece."

"Yeah, maybe." I took a dime out of my pocket and

tossed it over the fence like I was standing at the biggest wishing well in the world. The dime turned, over and over, as it fell. It flickered like a tiny silver spark all the way to the bottom.

Twenty-five

EVERY DAY, SCHOOL SEEMED less real. I went, I sat in classes, I failed tests, and I ate disgusting school lunches. I watched the other kids do what they always did. Fighting and gossip, flirting and goofing off, smoking in the lavs and beating up the geeks.

It was all perfectly normal. And it was all unreal, like I was stuck inside a movie and knew everyone was just an actor.

Kids did what they always did. Only it felt like they were just going through the motions. I swear I heard two girls near my locker talking but all that was coming out of their mouths was blah blah blah. No words, like they were extras in some crowd scene and the director had told them, "Just pretend to talk."

So school was nothing. Knacke was still out and I didn't see Frankengoon all week before the Bug Jar gig.

Up in Relly's attic, things were getting pretty tense.

We had three days till the gig and Butt had brought in a new tune he wanted us to do.

He showed up with an old album by Iggy and the Stooges. "It's called *Raw Power*. And that's the tune I want to do." He put the record on the turntable and out came this crude chugging riff. He started jerking his legs and whacking the side of his head in time. "Cool, right? Totally cool. These guys were like the grandfathers of punk."

The tune was simple. Relly and me had it down in about ten seconds. And Butt had even scribbled some of the words. The part that Jerod liked best was when he got to sing "Get down baby and kiss my feet."

We ran through it a couple of times. "So we do it at the Bug Jar, right?"

Relly shook his head. "I don't think so. It's getting too close to the gig. We've only got three days to go."

"It's done," Butt said. "We're ready, right? All Jerod's got to do is learn a couple of lines. Doesn't matter if he gets it all."

"I don't think so," Relly said.

"Come on. We're not doing a single tune I brought in. This one's easy and I love it. Raw Power!" he yelled. "The crowd will go nuts for it when Jerod gets to the chorus. Raw Power!"

"Let's save it for the next gig. We've already nailed down the set list."

"Yeah," Jerod said, "and you two figured it all out without even asking me."

"Maybe if you showed up on time once in a while, you'd get a say in the matter." Relly turned up his volume and let fly a long, fuzz-toned riff, silencing Jerod for the time being.

We sounded good. But still, all the little things that bugged Jerod were now ten times more obnoxious to him. He swore at me when I missed my cues. He picked up an empty pop can and threw it at Relly when his top E string broke. "What are you so bent about?" Relly snarled. "Strings break, OK? That's the way it goes." He looked over at me for support. "His Highness doesn't get it."

"Right!" Jerod yelled back. "So it's you two against me now. Well you better not forget that without me, you're just a couple of geek nothings. I can get guitar players as easy as I can get girls."

Butt threw a drumstick at him. And I figured in about ten seconds all three of them would start throwing punches. "Enough!" I shouted at them. "You're acting like six-year-olds."

Butt calmed down pretty fast. Relly and Jerod were still steaming. "We're all pretty stressed out," I said. "Why don't we take a break for a little while?"

Without saying another word, Jerod stormed out. Butt stayed behind his drums, adjusting the heads and tightening the stands for about the hundredth time.

I went downstairs with Relly and flopped onto the living room couch. Jerod was already out the door, revving his engine.

"You think he's quitting?" I asked.

Relly sneered. "He quits about once a month. There's always something bugging him. A while back he brought in this tune called 'Everybody Wants to Rule the World.' It was like a disco thing. Or one of those wimpy British synth bands. Duran Duran. Wham. Tears for Fears. God, I hate that stuff."

"And you just told him no?"

"It was perfect for him. He really does think he's the king of the world. But we're a metal band. It was totally not us."

Tannis came into the room. "Something wrong?" she said.

"Same old hissy fit from Jerod. He'll be back. He'll rip around the block a few times in his Acura. I don't know who he thinks he's showing off to. But he always comes back once he gets that crot out of his system."

Relly went to the bathroom and I was alone with his mom.

She pointed to a picture on the wall. Two girls, maybe my age. Back in the early '70s from the look of the hairstyles and the way the jeans were cut.

"That's me," Tannis said, pointing to one of the girls. "And that's my sister. Did Relly ever tell you about his aunt Lissa?"

"I don't think so."

I heard the toilet flush and then Relly's footsteps as he went back to the attic. As usual, it felt weird being alone with Tannis. But for once I didn't try to get away.

"We were only a year apart," Tannis said, taking the picture off the wall and handing it to me. "She was really into drama. You know: plays, theater. She was good. Very good."

"Does she still do it?" I asked. It was easy to see which one was Tannis. Darker hair, heavier features. Tannis, at least in the olden days, was kind of cute. But her sister was beautiful. "She's the one in the kitchen, right?" I said. "The zodiac picture. Aquarius."

"Yes, that's Lissa."

We heard a car door slam and then Jerod came stomping into the house. "So what are you waiting for?" he asked me. "Let's get back to work."

Just like Relly said, the fight was all forgotten. And if anything, we sounded even better after Jerod had his little tantrum.

No more talk about the set list. Relly had added the last tune, "Silence Loud," and that was that.

It was great, better, I bet, than any drug. So much

power, so much joy blasting out of the amps. Relly faced in toward the drums. And me, too. With Jerod in the middle. We were a perfect four, banging our heads against the air.

Afterward, I wondered what the real Silence Loud would've thought if she'd heard us. She was a pioneer girl from the olden days. She died when she was seventeen years old. That's what her stone said. Probably she'd run screaming from the room if she heard her song. I felt a little bad about that, stealing her name. Maybe in a hundred years somebody would steal mine too, thinking, *Zee, that's the weirdest name I ever heard.*

I was OK with that though. And I hoped Silence would understand if I ever met her and had to explain it all.

Twenty-six

WE HAULED OUR GEAR TO the Bug Jar in Butt's van. *Just like a real band,* I thought. *This is what it will be like when we tour. The four of us together, all cranked up, ready for the stage, hungry for the almighty noise.*

Only when we got big, we'd have roadies and the places would be huge.

The Bug Jar holds maybe a hundred people. In the front room, a gigantic fly rotates from the ceiling above the bar. There's seedy old punks and a few biker types, college kids and teenagers drinking pop. Even though we were playing that night, we had to have our hands stamped with Xs. No beer for Scorpio Bone.

Kruel and Unusual was already there, hanging around the bar. For a big-name act, they were pretty friendly. The lead singer talked a little with Relly, about mikes and amps.

So we set up and watched the crowd come in. By the

time we were supposed to go on, the place was packed. The back room is where the stage is. There's a booth for the sound man and about as much room on the dance floor as in Relly's kitchen. In the back was a table where one of the Kruel and Unusual girlfriends was selling CDs and band T-shirts. By eleven o'clock we could hardly get through the crowd to the stage.

"All right," Jerod yelled, grabbing the mike stand with both hands. "We are Scorpio Bone and this is the end of the world as you know it." Butt gave us the four-count and off we went.

How good were we? Better than ever. How did the crowd like us? They screamed for three encores, and that's saying something for the opening band. Everyone came to see Kruel and Unusual, but they went away talking about Scorpio Bone.

We did all our best songs, which means all the ones I wrote the words to. With the crowd pushing up against the stage, with the noise ripping out of the amps like a horde of furious demons, with Jerod yelling my words, I thought nothing could ever be as good.

My Ibanez and me were like one body. And Relly's crushing riffs were mine too. Butt's bass drum pulsed in my brain. Jerod screamed words that I had written, or copied off old gravestones. And the whole crowd was mixed up in our rising, roaring tide.

I was back behind Relly and Jerod. Still, it felt like this was *my* night, not anyone else's. This was for me, and me alone. This was what I'd been waiting all those years for. To be real, to be wild and loud and free. And to have a hundred people yelling because they loved it.

Twenty-seven

FOR THE FIRST TIME, I truly got what the band was about. Each one of us had joined for a different reason. And each of us got a different payoff. Jerod could stand before the crowd like a pagan idol to be worshiped. Every girl in the place wanted to be with him. And every guy wanted his look, his moves, his voice, his godlike glow.

Butt wanted to smash and pound, like he had a Mack truck in each of his hands. Diesel engine stink, noise, and raw power.

Relly had his Ghost Metal.

And me?

I wanted to be part of something bigger than myself. And I got that. Of course, I also wanted to be near Relly. But the real payoff that night was to hear my words huge and heavy, blasting out of the speakers. Jerod sang and shouted, yelled and yowled. Only it was me, not him, the crowd was listening to. For once, my voice was really and truly heard.

We came down off the stage and it was like we really were gods. I mean, I still didn't understand about tetrads and ancient, secret powers. But this made sense. People loved us. We'd grabbed them and shook them and they wanted more. We didn't have to burst into flame or make the rains come. This was the real magic power. Bass, drums, guitar, and a voice. That's all we needed to be gods.

What happened right after is all a blur. I was so cranked up I hardly knew who I was. But I do know that Kruel and Unusual actually heard our set and they were just as stoked as the crowd. The singer asked Relly if we could do some more shows with them, in other towns. He talked about real money. Not just a little handful of sweaty five-dollar bills.

Then he said his manager was there and did we want to talk?

So we squeezed our way out of the back room and headed for a table. "He loved your set," the Kruel and Unusual drummer said. "He wants to talk about where you guys are heading."

I took one look and froze. This manager was a creepy-looking guy with mirror sunglasses on. He had a drink in front of him and a ring on every finger.

"It's Scratch," I said to Relly. I felt my stomach turning and my legs starting to wobble. "It's Scratch. This was all a setup."

The place was so noisy, Relly didn't hear a word I said. I kind of hung back, fear gnawing at my brain. "Don't," I said. "Don't go over there." I reached for Relly, but couldn't hold him.

Relly went and so did Jerod. I guess Butt was still enjoying all the high-fives and backslapping.

"No," I groaned. "Don't."

Then the manager guy took off his glasses and relief flooded through me. No bulgy eye like Scratch. He said, "You were great, really something," and his voice wasn't the one I'd heard on the phone and on the bridge.

He stood up and he was way over six feet tall. "You could fill a place ten times bigger than this," he said. "A hundred times."

He shook Relly's hand. The crowd pushed me closer and he took mine too. I felt like a little kid again, playing at being a grownup. He held onto my hand. And my sickening dread all drained away. "I'm Ray Kola." He spelled it.

"I'm Zee," I said.

"Cool name." When he smiled, gold glittered in his mouth.

It wasn't Scratch in disguise, after all. Ray Kola was really his name and he really was a manager. I heard him talking with Relly about better gigs. I just let go then and kind of drifted, like this all was a perfect dream.

The fear was gone. Everything was going to be OK.

It was three in the morning when Butt finally dropped me off at my house.

Twenty-eight

AT FOUR THIRTY THE phone rang. I staggered down the hall and grabbed it. "Yeah?"

It was Tannis and she wanted to know where Relly was.

"He was hanging around outside the Bug Jar with Kruel and Unusual when I took off. The gig went great."

"He never came home," she said. "I called Jonathan and Jerod. He's not with them either." The panic in Tannis's voice brought me totally awake in a hurry.

"He's not with you?" she asked.

"No!" I was almost yelling. "Butt took me home about three."

"They must have got him, Zee." Though she'd never mentioned their names before, I knew she meant Knacke and the others. "They've taken him hostage."

"What are you talking about?" I shouted. It didn't matter how loud I got. My dad could sleep through an H-bomb attack.

"I know it! I just know it! They've taken him prisoner. Knacke and Franken and Scratch."

"Why would they do such a thing?" She didn't answer me. "Did you call the police? Or how about the hospitals? Maybe he was in an accident."

I felt like I was living in two different worlds at the same time. In the normal one, we were just kids in a band. In the other one, which seemed to get more real every day, the rules were all different. The police couldn't do a thing against living human fire. Teachers were maniac wizards. The assistant principal of the school was also the mastermind of a kidnapping ring.

"Relly was talking with a guy called Ray Kola. He manages Kruel and Unusual. Maybe they're still talking."

"It's almost five, Zee. The sun will be up soon. It's not this manager guy. It's Knacke and the others. I just know it."

I sat in the kitchen for an hour, watching the numbers flick away on the oven clock. Slowly, a watery dawn light filled the room. Tannis didn't call again. At six thirty I got ready for school. My dad was still sleeping when I went out to get the bus.

Twenty-nine

SCHOOL WAS ACTUALLY A good thing that day. At least at first. I mean it was normal. Boring, yeah. A waste of time, yeah. But it was something I could count on.

Butt didn't come in. I figured he'd been out all night.

And Relly never showed, so I was back to the way it used to be. All alone, kind of floating silently around the edges of the crowds. Some kids told me how much they liked our show. Mostly, though, I was back to being a stranger and a loner again.

Of course, going to bio was the worst. Relly wasn't there. And Knacke was back.

He did a lesson about lava and magma that day. On the desk was a miniature volcano. After the lights were all out, he tossed something in the hole and soon a weird reddish light was rising up. Then glowing orange ooze poured out the top, across the desk, and down to the floor in bright gooey trails.

I just sat there in a daze and Knacke left me alone.

Until the bell rang and the others all rushed out.

I was at the end of the line. Knacke stationed himself at the door. As the last kid went out, Knacke cut off my escape.

"We need to talk, Zee."

I didn't argue. No point in fighting him now. Without Relly with me, I had no strength to resist.

"You're aware that Relly is not in school today?"

No point in answering.

"You understand that he's with us now."

"He's fire," I said. "You already got fire. Scratch said you wanted me, not him. You need a watergod, not fire."

"That's correct. And that is why we're having this little talk now, Zee. Scratch made you an offer, which you foolishly ignored. And so we've had to add a little inducement. It's really very simple, Zee." He kept saying my name, stretching it out, savoring the sound. That made my helpless feeling ten times worse.

"It's simple. You join us and make our tetrad complete again. Four and no more, forever more." He smiled his disgusting smile. "You join us and Relly will go free."

"And if I don't?"

"Then you'll never see your friend again. And nor will anyone else. Simple, really. Very simple."

"Join you?"

I remembered a math teacher saying once, "There are

no stupid questions." Maybe he was right, but I sure felt stupid then. Join Knacke and the others? Did they have a band? This almost made me laugh. Maybe they played weddings. Or did corny old country stuff. "Lost Highway," "Your Cheatin' Heart," that kind of stuff. Maybe they needed a bass player.

"Yes, join us. Four and no more, and we'll be restored."

"I'm just a kid."

"We understand that, Zee. But you're also a god. You know that. We know that. And we need you." He sucked in air, like a smoker fighting to catch his breath.

"There was a fourth once, who made our tetrad complete. Surely Relly must have told you about this. We had all we needed. We were supposed to be four forever more. But she's gone now, and that's why we need you, Zee."

"Stop saying that, all right?" It was like my name gave him power over me. "Just stop saying it!"

"Fine, fine. If you need some time, I understand. But you'll have to deal with this soon enough."

Then he stabbed both of his hands into the puddle of glowing liquid. And he held them out, as if offering me a handful of molten gold.

"Join us, and you'll know power a hundred times greater than with your little kiddy friends. We're mature, seasoned by time, you might say. We have so much more to offer. Do you want to die? Or do you want to live forever, Zee?"

"But Relly said that—"

"Relly is a strutting fool. He has barely an inkling of how things truly are. He doesn't have the strength or the wisdom or the courage to be immortal. All he cares about is his idiotic rock band. Sooner or later his tetrad would fall to pieces. And then where would you be? But we will be together forever. Franken and Scratch and Knacke and Zee."

"Shut up!" I yelled, and pushed past him to the door.

"We'll talk later," he said. "You know how to reach me."

Thirty

I GOT OFF THE BUS at Slime Street. Tannis opened the door without me even knocking. She must've been watching from the kitchen window.

"Knacke said he wants to trade," I told her. "He wants me to join him and the other two." I slumped down at the table, head in both hands. "He said Relly can go free if I just join them. That's all. Join up with three ugly, poxy, smelly old men. He said if I don't, no one will ever see Relly again."

Tannis groaned and her face went gray. "I knew it. I knew it," she murmured. She clutched at the countertop.

"I'm sorry," I said. "It's all my fault."

If I hadn't joined Scorpio Bone, then none of this would've happened. If I'd just stayed all by myself, then Relly would be safe now. "I really am sorry. I shouldn't ever have talked to him."

I don't know what I expected her to say. But she didn't disagree. She didn't come right out and blame me. She didn't need to. I was doing that just fine all by myself.

"We've got to get him back," she said as she sat down beside me and took my hands in hers. No mention of the police. What good would they do? Again I had the dizzy feeling that I was living in two worlds. Yeah, police and courts and jails existed here. Tannis could pick up the phone and report her son missing. But I wasn't sure Relly was even in the same world as all that now.

"What do you want me to do?" I asked. If somebody I could trust just told me, it would be so much easier. My dad? yeah, right. He'd be a ton of help. Other teachers? As far as I knew they all were in on this, one huge secret kid-destroying club.

"I've feared this day since he was born," Tannis said. "I knew it was coming. I knew they'd come to steal him away." She clutched at my hands. Her voice trembled. "They'll do anything to get what they want."

"You know Knacke?"

"For what seems like my entire life," she whispered. "He's been out there, waiting."

"So you were the one before me?"

She shook her head.

"I asked Relly if Knacke's fourth element was a girl. And he said she was."

Tannis sighed, then asked, "How much has Relly told you?"

"I have no idea. How much is there to tell?"

She let go of my hands and stood. "Wait here," she said. She came back from the living room a minute later carrying a picture frame.

"This is me. Do you understand?" The photo showed Tannis, maybe sixteen years old, standing at an iron railing. Behind her was a huge rushing river. And just to the side was the edge. "Niagara Falls. In the spring of 1973. My sister took this picture. Then she gave me the camera and we switched places. But that picture is gone. Long gone. I'd give anything to have that picture again. She did modeling, lots of ads and calendar work. But no picture ever captured her like the one I took that day at Niagara Falls."

"It was her? Relly's aunt? She was the one?"

"Yes. She was the one. Knacke claimed her not long after that picture was taken. Only a month or two. That's why I wish I had it again. It showed Lissa before. Lissa free. Lissa like she was supposed to be. Not tangled up with Knacke's fire."

"She was his watergod?"

"For years."

"And Relly knows all this?" I asked.

"Most of it. I told him what he needed to know. Since he was a little boy, he knew who he was, where he came from, where he's going."

"So what happened to your sister?"

No answer.

"Is she still alive?"

The word "No" came quiet as a breath.

"Did Knacke . . . I mean, was your sister . . . How did she die?"

Tannis sighed again, and I thought she was going to tell me the whole story. But she went back to Relly. "We've got to get him back."

"How?"

"Give them what they want. It's our only chance. You care about Relly. I know that, Zee. Give Knacke what he wants and you'll save your best friend's life."

I wanted to say, *What about my life?* But I just sat there, looking at the pictures. Lissa had been part of Knacke's four and now she was dead. Everyone, Knacke and Tannis and maybe even Relly, wanted me to join the four. *What about my life?* The question kept asking itself in my head. The room was silent for a long time.

Thirty-one

SCHOOL ASSEMBLIES WERE usually OK. I mean, yeah, they're totally stupid. But we get to skip a class or two. Drug awareness, sex and safety, anger management: they're all the same. We all just veg out and watch the minutes crawl past. I swear the year before they even brought in this guy who was a world-famous whistler. They thought we'd be thrilled to hear his versions of TV commercial themes mixed in with birdcalls.

So I marched with all the other zombie kids into the aud, expecting nothing.

There was Frankengoon himself, up onstage. And around him were these big shiny posters. One said, "Don't Cloud Your Mind with Negative Thoughts." Another proclaimed, "Be Your Best Self Every Day."

Frankengoon fiddled with the mike. Of course, he made it feed back, wild screeches coming from the speakers. When he got the PA under control and all the classes were settled down, he started in.

"There's a lot of bad thinking going on these days. And it's about time we turn that around."

They had the cheerleaders lined up in front of the stage. And every time Frankengoon paused, they jumped up to pump up the crowd. It worked about as well as CPR on roadkill. We all sat there bored, annoyed, squirming as our assistant principal yelled about School Spirit and Positive Thinking.

I was about ready to scream. Relly was gone, maybe even dead. They'd grabbed him and whisked him away to some secret hiding place. And here I was listening to Frankengoon talk like a TV preacher. He was a monster, a vicious, horrible old man. And he was telling us to "Look on the bright side," and "Keep your eyes open for ways to help out."

Though there were hundreds of kids packed into the aud, it felt like he was looking straight at me. "We're going to put a stop to all this stinking thinking!" he declared. "It's time to rev up your positive energy and get motorvated."

I closed my eyes and tried to shut out his voice. I thought about rain, about fire and wind and deep black earth. Right then, at that very moment, Relly might be getting killed by Knacke's secret science. Maybe they had his head floating in a jar of green goo. And what was I doing? Sitting in school, listening to Frankengoon's fake optimist crot.

Way off, I felt water moving. Underground, there's

supposed to be rivers. Huge streams that never see the light of day. I plunged my mind downward, into those dark, hidden places. I tried to escape the aud, the school, the so-called real world, and go down into the regions of underground water.

Frankengoon was complaining now about "bad influences." Did this mean our music? Maybe. He told us we should all "turn away from darkness to the light." I thought he was talking then right to me. Cheerleaders: good. Scorpio Bone: bad. School spirit: good. Ghost Metal: very bad.

I kept my mind pushing downward. I felt the water, the black lakes deep inside the earth.

Every lie he told, every bogus line about "being positive," made the feeling in me stronger. I couldn't shut him up. I couldn't escape or do a thing to save Relly. So I turned inside myself, following the black, writhing currents.

Behind me I heard muttering. Then somebody stood up. Kids were turning around in their seats. For a second I thought it was Relly, bursting down the door and surging in full flame toward the stage.

I opened my eyes and looked. No flames, no light, no Relly.

Still, kids were moving around, talking and trying to get their teachers' attention.

My fists were tight as padlocks. My stomach was turning and coiling. My brain was still in the underground places. Water, water, endless black water.

Then Frankengoon finally saw what was happening.

There was a stream running right down the aud's main aisle. A shiny snake of water was heading for the stage.

Teachers started getting up, trying to make their kids move away from the flood.

Now it came from the sides too, water pouring in from every doorway. Some kids were jumping up on their seats. Others were stamping their feet in the widening puddles. I heard a steady pouring noise and knew then that every sink in the school was running over. Every toilet was overflowing and even the showers down in the gym wing were running full blast.

Soon enough it was like a wet riot. Kids were splashing every which way. Teachers were yelling. The stream reached the front of the aud and Frankengoon started screaming into the mike. "Order! Order!" His voice boomed like a judge. "Exit in an orderly fashion!"

I got up and followed my row. It was amazing to see the little river running down the aisle. Black water with a mind of its own. I turned to look back just as I reached the exit. As the current ran around my feet, I felt strength running into me. As the crowd pushed past, I was steady as a rock in a rushing river. I looked toward the stage. Frankengoon was silent now, gripping the podium like it was a life raft from a sinking ship.

He saw me. He stared. He was so filled with hate he was almost glowing.

I turned and let the flood of bodies swirl me out of the aud. The fire department was already there. Guys in huge floppy boots were rushing around with hoses. The exit lights were all flashing. And the stream poured on, from every lav and shower and drinking fountain in the school.

Thirty-two

I FOUND BUTT IN the parking lot. "Let's go," I said. He got in his van and opened the passenger door. I climbed in. "It's all happening. You understand? They took Relly as a hostage. They want me. We've got to fight back, rescue him."

Butt nodded. "So where are we going?"

"You understand what's going on, right?" I'd never actually talked with Butt about who and what we were. "Knacke's grabbed Relly for a hostage. They want me to join their tetrad." He nodded again. I guess Relly had explained it all to him. Or maybe Butt wasn't as dimwitted as he acted.

"How long have you known?" I asked. "I mean about being—"

"The god of dirt?" He smiled, kind of sheepish. "When I was a little kid they couldn't keep me out of the mud. One time I filled the bathtub with dirt when nobody was home. I turned it into mud and played in it for hours.

They beat me, I mean bad. Mr. Belt came out and I was crying all night. Still, I kept going back."

He put the key in the slot and twisted it to make his motor roar to life. "I was nine when I got my first drums. That was all it took. I could drub them hard as my old man beat me. Harder. I could put all that hate into my hands and pound the skins and it felt better than anything in the world."

"That's why you joined Relly?"

"Blam!" he said, punching his fists into the air. "I just want to make the biggest noise in the whole world. I want to hit and hit hard."

"What about the—"

"Relly told me about tetrads and elements and stuff. I get it, I guess. Or maybe I'm too stupid to really—"

"You're not stupid."

"OK, sure. I'm not stupid. The point is, I don't care much about Relly's weird stuff. All I know is he plays like nobody I've ever heard. And when the four of us are together it's amazing, like we're breaking on through."

I got what he meant, even if I wouldn't have put it that way.

"Something opens up. A door, a window. I don't know. Jerod gets it, too. Only, all he cares about is looking good and having people rave about him." Butt started the motor. The whole van rattled and throbbed.

We pulled out and edged past a fire truck. Hundreds of kids were milling around, talking, huddling, trying to keep warm.

"Where we going?" Butt said.

"Knacke's house," I told him. "I looked him up in the phone book. He lives out by the airport. Just the other side of the canal."

Thirty-three

IT WAS A NORMAL-LOOKING HOUSE. But it was all alone in a neighborhood of giant gas tanks, rent-a-car lots, and rusty, abandoned machines. Nearby, about a hundred railroad cars waited on weed-infested tracks.

We turned onto Knacke's street and a jet went over, so close my teeth rattled.

"You sure this is right?" Butt asked. "He's got a good job. He could live in a way better place than this."

"Maybe he likes to be alone," I said.

All around his house were empty lots. "Maybe this was a good neighborhood in the olden days. Probably everyone else sold out. But he hung on 'cause nobody will bother him here." Even with the windows rolled up, I could smell nasty fumes. Jet exhaust, or spills from the gas tanks.

"Now what?" Butt asked.

"Knacke's still at school."

"So we just go in the front door?"

"I don't know. Gimmee a minute to think." The Buttmobile had no heat. The longer we sat there doing nothing, the worse it got. Already, my feet were numb.

"If they kidnapped Relly then it's not against the law to go in there and save him, right?"

Butt shrugged. "It's probably breaking and entering."

"That doesn't matter though, right? We came here to save Relly."

He shut off the motor and we went up the crumbling driveway. Another jet went over. The huge roaring shadow sliced across Knacke's yard.

The screaming thunder dwindled down. But a growling kept on, even after the plane had landed. "Crot Almighty," Butt groaned.

He'd seen the dog first, a huge, shiny, black monster with raging purple-red eyes. I stood there, frozen, as the beast lunged. He stopped, snapped back in midair, at the end of his chain. This made him even madder, and now my fear was like poison pumping through my veins.

"Let's go, let's go!" Butt yelled, running for the van.

I was sick with fear, ready to throw up. Still, I didn't back away. "We came to save Relly," I yelled. "I'm not going home without him."

The dog's chain was long, and as he raced back and forth, it dragged in the frosty stubble of grass. He lunged again, jerked back again, and then bolted to one side.

Butt dodged back. We were safe. Only we couldn't get near the house.

The monster dog ran from side to side, and everywhere his paws touched the ground, he left a puff of steam. Was he a creature of fire like Knacke? Was that stinking steam that blew from his nostrils just breath, or smoke from some inner fires?

"We can stop him," I said. "Water and earth. You and me together. Water and earth makes mud."

I thought of rain and the rivers coursing underground. I thought of endless water, and the ground under the dog's feet became softer. Butt saw what I was doing, and I guess he turned his thoughts inside, too. The god of dirt and the god of water, making Knacke's yard into a lake of raw mud.

The dog was stuck, jerking and twisting, trying to get free. His legs were sinking into the ground. His paws were gone now, deeper and deeper.

"All right," I whispered. "Stop." I let go of the watery thoughts.

The ground, which had been frozen till we made it soft, went back the way it was. The dog was trapped, all four legs buried in the rock-hard earth.

"Now! Let's move!" I said. We ran up the driveway to the front door.

"We'll just go in fast, get Relly free, and then we're gone. Two minutes, that's all it'll take," I said.

I grabbed the doorknob and another plane came in, close enough I could have hit it if I threw a rock straight up. My teeth rattled, and so did the screen door. The booming went way lower all of a sudden. I heard the plane hit the runway as I twisted the doorknob.

Like a hundred-pound fist, another dog slammed out of nowhere. The huge jaws snapped and slavered, about an inch from my face. There was glass between us, and I guess that's all that kept me from getting my eyes torn out of my head.

Butt was swearing, I was screaming, the dogs were snarling, one behind and one in front.

Again the dog inside threw himself at the glass door. Flames shot out of his nostrils. Smoke and ash were swirling around his head.

Butt grabbed me by the shoulder and got me away from the door.

We ran for the van. By the time Butt had the motor going, the dog in the yard was free. He bolted toward us. His chain stopped him dead in midair again. Butt put on the gas and we were gone, with the scream of jets and the wild yapping of Knacke's fire dogs chasing us down the road.

Thirty-four

TWO MINUTES LATER WE got pulled over by the police.

Butt could swear with the best of them. And while we waited there, watching the flashing red light in the mirror, Butt reeled off every curse he knew. "I'm gonna lose my license. I know it, I just know it." His hands were tight on the wheel, so tight I thought he'd bend it up like a pretzel.

Finally, the officer got out of his car and came toward us. *It's one of them,* I thought. *They're everywhere. The assistant principal at school, the police, probably the mayor and every priest and preacher in the city, too. They're all part of this.*

He came up beside the van. "Your license and registration," he said. I tried to get a good look, but he stood behind us. All I could see was the glint of his mirror shades.

"Crot Almighty," Butt hissed when the officer went back to his car. "I have my license for a week and it gets yanked."

I was thinking, *We have way bigger things than your*

license to worry about. They still have Relly and they won't
hesitate to kill him if we don't do as they tell us.

"I wasn't speeding," Butt said. "I'm positive I wasn't
speeding."

"It doesn't matter now. They got you."

The officer was taking forever, which made it all the
worse for Butt. Finally, he couldn't stand it anymore and
got out of the van. Instantly a voice boomed from the
police car loudspeaker, "Get back in your vehicle. Now!"

Butt did as he was told, and started punching his fist
against the dashboard.

At last, the officer came back.

"I wasn't speeding," Butt snapped. "You know I wasn't
speeding." He was clutching at the steering wheel so hard
his knuckles were white.

"That's correct. However, your brake lights are not
functioning and your side door mirror is missing." There
was a rusty hole where the mirror had been attached.

"Listen," I said, leaning across Butt to see the officer.
"We have a friend who's been kind of . . . we think that
someone's kidnapped him."

The officer handed Butt his ticket. "You have seven
days to bring this vehicle into compliance."

"Honest," I said. "We need some help. A guy from school,
he's this insane teacher." I tried to see the policeman's face.
"And he's kidnapped our friend. Is there anything you can—"

"Get your brake lights repaired today. And the mirror replaced."

I kept talking, asking for help, almost pleading. It was like I wasn't even there. Like no sound was coming out of my mouth.

Butt pushed me back to my side of the seat.

"Have a nice day," the policeman said in a voice as dead as a robot's. And with that, he went back to his car.

Thirty-five

I TOLD BUTT TO DRIVE to the Chimes Diner. "I think my dad's working now."

What was my plan? To ask him to fix everything? What was I going to say? "I know I haven't seen you in days, but I thought maybe you could figure out a way to rescue Relly." Or: "The police are no use, and everyone at school is involved, too. So you're my last hope for help."

I don't know what I expected. Still, we went in and I asked Mary Kay, the lady at the cash register, if my dad was there.

Rubbing at the nasty red spot on her cheek, she said, "I think so." Her hair always kind of scared me. It was big and hard-looking, like a bees' nest made out of copper wire. "Go on back and ask."

So we did. Dickey, one of the prep guys, gave me a big smile and said I looked all grown up. "Haven't seen you in here in months. You too good for us now?" He was standing at a steel sink full of wings, ice, and chicken blood.

I felt kind of sick. The smells of the kitchen were thick as fog. Sizzling grease and mop water, a bucket of raw onions and bubbling pot of red sauce. "Is my dad here? I need to talk to him."

Dickey shrugged. "Haven't seen him in a while."

We wandered around the kitchen, then to the back stockroom. I even had Butt check the men's lav.

Mr. Poole, the manager, poked his head out from his tiny office. "He's not on till six tonight. He's got the last shift."

"We could wait," Butt said.

I gave up. "No point. Let's go."

Thirty-six

I'M NOT SURE WHY, but we ended up back at Relly's. The house looked even more like a ruined tower that day, tall and spindly between the two empty lots. Butt parked on the street and we sat a while as the last light faded from the sky.

Slime Street was even deader than usual. A few lone leaves rattled on the maple trees. A black VW beetle crawled by. Its tailpipe dragged on the road, spitting sparks. When the rattling had gone to nothing, I got out of the van.

"You coming in?"

Butt shook his head. "I better get going." I knew no one at his house cared when he came or went. No—it was just that he wanted to get away from me. "Gimme a call if you get any ideas."

"Right. Sure." I slammed the van door, maybe too hard. Flecks of rust rained down around my feet. "See you later."

He drove off and I went up the steps to Relly's front door.

Like before, Tannis opened up without me knocking. She looked worse than I felt. Her shoulders kind of sagged. Her skin was almost gray, like she'd been sick for a month. "You're back." I could barely make out the words, she was so quiet.

"And you failed."

I nodded. "Completely. Nobody's going to help us."

"Then you have to do what they want." She never once said it was all my fault. Still, I knew what she was thinking. *You made this mess. Now it's your job to clean it up. You've got to answer for what you've done.*

"We've got to get him back," she whispered.

"I know. I know." I climbed to the attic, up one flight, two flights, of creaking steps. The light was already on, the one bare bulb that dangled above the practice space. Relly's guitar case was open. The Strat shone a brilliant blood red.

The wind was whipping at the roof. Drafts and even a few little fingers of snow came in through the cracks around the rafters. The house kind of moaned, like it was dreaming, making sad noises in its sleep.

I looked around slowly at the practice space. Pop cans, heaps of cable, some broken drumsticks, a pizza box, shredded guitar picks, candy wrappers, scraps of paper where Relly had scrawled words and chords. Flattening one page out, I read,

Now deep in earth, this bed of sighs,
I wait till I, like fire, shall rise.
In latter days, the healing rain
shall wash away these tears of pain.
Then will my voice in great goodbyes
join to the chorus of the skies.

It was in Relly's handwriting. He must've copied it down on one of our Mount Hope trips. Below the poem was the name Silence Loud, and then her dates. Seventeen years old when she died.

I tried to picture Silence. I tried to look backward through time to see the girl whose name seemed so weird and yet so perfectly right. She was long, long gone. Still, it was like I could almost hear her talking. "Then will my voice, in great goodbyes." I was reading the grave poem aloud. I was hearing Silence, making Silence appear in the cold empty practice space. "Join to the chorus of the skies."

Tannis was coming up the steps. I wadded the paper and stuffed it into my pocket. She emerged from the shadows carrying a big book. "I want to show you something," she said.

She lay the book down and opened it. Pictures, hundreds of pictures. Relly as a baby, a toddler, a ten-year-old, a teenager. It didn't matter how young he was, I could tell it was him every time. Those big eyes, staring so intense, so full of longing. Even when he was little, he knew he was totally different. And he wanted something better than the nothing of school and TV and malls and crowds of other kids.

Tannis was sort of crying. And I was heading there fast. It was like Relly was already dead. Here we were, the two people who loved him the most, sharing a last moment before we said goodbye to him.

"The first time," Tannis said, sniffing, "the first time Relly felt the power, we'd been up to Seabreeze. He went on all the rides. He loved going there. Round and round. Up and down. He'd just come off the Jackrabbit and he was so excited. He wanted to get right back on. He was so happy. Then he felt the power. And we looked and there was light flickering around his hand. He got scared. So did I. Terrified, actually. And then the flame came. Just his hand, that day. Just a ball of fire at the end of his arm."

She pointed to a picture of Relly at the amusement park. He was maybe eight or nine. Long black hair, big inky eyes. I couldn't tell what he was feeling. Maybe joy, maybe fear. Something too strong to control.

"The power came and the flames were there in his hand." Tannis wiped her nose again. "We never went back to Seabreeze. He loved that place. But after that, he said he never wanted to go back."

She was about to close the picture album, but I held back her hand. "What's this one?" I asked.

"That's up at Durand." The picture showed a strip of sandy beach, people in the water, boats way off.

I felt all weak suddenly, quaking like I was a brass gong and Butt had just given me a good whack. No shimmering sound was coming from my body. Still, from head to toe and hand to hand, a steady shiver was passing through me.

There was Relly at the beach. And behind, there was me, Zee, up to my knees in the waves. He was facing the camera. Not smiling. He never smiled in these pictures. And I was just behind, facing out toward the huge blue horizon. The picture showed him full face. I was in profile.

There it was, proof. We might not have known each other before. But our paths had crossed years ago. We'd been to the beach on the same day. I knew exactly how old I was in that picture because I could remember the Black Sabbath T-shirt I was wearing. Somebody stole it in gym class that year. It was my favorite and it got robbed from my locker in seventh grade.

"That's me," I said.

"What?"

"There. In the picture. Look." I pointed to myself, a skinny pale girl in a purple and black T-shirt.

"My God," Tannis murmured.

It was just coincidence, right? OK, so once a few years ago, Relly and me had been on the same strip of Durand beach. What was the big deal? We lived in the same city. Why wouldn't we go to the same park on the same summer day?

The picture showed me looking out at the vastness of the water. I didn't remember that trip to the beach. I guess my dad had taken me on a hot August afternoon. But it was totally gone from my mind. All that remained was my memory of that T-shirt.

I looked very sad in the picture, like I'd lost my best friend. Only my best friend was standing right there close enough to touch. I didn't know it, of course. I didn't notice the scrawny kid with the big dark eyes. We were a couple feet apart and didn't have a clue that in a few years we'd meet again. That Scorpio Bone would happen. That we'd be part of the four and no more. That Knacke and the others would tear us apart.

It was the saddest thing I ever saw, that picture. There I was, looking so miserable, so alone. And there was my best-friend-to-be, just a few feet away. I could've just turned and seen him and gotten talking. He could've turned and seen my T-shirt and asked me about music. But no, that didn't happen, and so I had to wait years before we'd meet again.

A couple of weeks together. And then separate again. The best couple weeks of my life.

I took a last look around the practice space. I figured I'd never see it again. Butt's drum set, Jerod's mike stand, Relly's Strat, beautiful as fire. My Ibanez was at home.

"You can save his life, Zee."

I kicked a pop can into the shadows.

"Give Knacke what he wants. Please. Save him."

"First tell me what happened to your sister."

Tannis took a deep breath. "She died seven years ago. Knacke's been waiting, searching, ever since. He's getting desperate. If he doesn't complete the tetrad soon, he'll die. All of them will die."

"What about Lissa?"

"She joined Knacke when she was about your age. The rest of her life she was part of that four."

"I don't get it. In the pictures, she's beautiful. Not a poxy old hag. She looks like a good person. Not a—"

"She was good! Maybe too good."

"What does that mean?"

"She was an actress. She went to New York for a little while and got in some plays. Off Broadway. Those are the ones that hardly pay a nickel. She was the hopeless romantic. Ophelia was her best part, the girl who loved Hamlet.

"But she came back here. She rejoined Knacke and for the rest of her life she was his watergod. When it finally got too much, she took her own life." Tannis's voice got weaker, quieter. "Into the river."

"Niagara Falls? Like in the picture?"

"No. Right here. On the Broad Street bridge. She climbed up the rail and went over. She couldn't stand being with him anymore. So she went back. To her element. Just as she said she would. In a minute or two she was dragged by the current to the upper falls. A hundred feet straight down. They never found her body."

"And you want me to—"

"You can save his life."

"I know. I know. But what about *my* life? Am I going to end up the same as your sister? Why did she do it? I mean, why kill herself after being part of Knacke's four for so long?"

"Because of Relly. It was right after the time at Seabreeze. When the power came down on him. Lissa suspected he had the power all along. But then it happened and it was too much for her. Being part of Knacke's four was bad enough. But to know that it was in the family. That was too much."

Tannis grabbed my hands. "It started when we were your age, Zee. He claimed her—that's how he put it. He claimed her when she was a teenager. And for ten years she was a part of it. Totally lost. I mean, we kept in touch, but she was lost to me as a sister.

"There's more, a lot more to Knacke than you've seen, Zee. And Lissa got pulled all the way into it. But when the power came down on Relly, then something changed. Maybe she felt guilty and that's what finally got her. I still don't understand it completely. Maybe it was shame. Or fear that it would go on forever. But when it was clear that the power had been passed to the next generation, Lissa couldn't take it anymore.

"Ever since she was your age, she was way too deep into the Ophelia thing. And you know what happens to her, right? Crazy, then suicide. Lissa always said that's how it would end. 'Baptism' is what she called it. Baptized into death. 'The most beautiful way to die.' That's what she always said."

The words were coming out of Tannis in a flood, fast and powerful.

"So she went to the bridge."

I jerked my hands free. "All right! All right. Enough."

Without really thinking, I grabbed up some of Butt's broken sticks, and the pages where Relly had scrawled some lyrics for songs we never finished.

I went downstairs to the kitchen and found the phone book. "Festus B. Knacke," I read aloud.

It took me three tries to get the number right. My fingers were shaking, I guess. My eyes were out of focus. Maybe it was tears.

"Hello?"

"It's me, Zee. I made up my mind. You'll set Relly free if I join you, right? No tricks. He's free and he's safe. Right? It's just me you want."

"Of course. I am a man of my word. You know that, Zee."

"OK. Then I agree to join. You set Relly free and I'll make your four."

fire

earth

wind

water

Part Three

One

I SAID IT STARTS WITH FIRE. And fire led me to the end, too.

I made a little goodbye backyard blaze. Scraps of paper, splintered drumsticks, fliers for some upcoming shows. I cleared a space in my dad's barbeque and set it all burning.

By the time I'd gotten home that terrible day it was near dusk. There was serious weather coming in, the first real storm of the year.

I'm used to snow, but this felt different. The cold was colder. The wind was meaner. And the skies, when the clouds swirled off, had this weird red glow. A wild sunset, with big churning masses of purple and scarlet streaks like bloody sword blades.

First I got the crumpled pages of Relly's lyrics burning. Then I added some dead leaves and the Scorpio Bone fliers. As the paper caught fire, the pictures on the fliers twisted like overcooked bacon. I put on Butt's broken drumsticks, some leftover charcoal, and then a piece of wood that had blown off our sugar maple.

The wind pushed at the fire, threatened to snuff it right out. But the little red and orange flickers grew. And soon the wind kind of joined the blaze rather than fighting it and breathed in life. I collected more sticks and some scrap wood out of the garage.

Soon enough I had a real wind-whipped bonfire.

The last thing I added was my notebook. Inside were my favorite poems from Mount Hope, and drawings and scribbles. There even was one page stained purple and wrinkly where Relly had spilled some of his Panther Blood.

This was hard. Maybe even harder than calling Knacke that last time. Even if Scorpio Bone never played again, the notebook would be proof that we were real once upon a time. We never recorded even one song. And I guess soon enough all the kids who'd seen our shows would forget. Other bands would come along. Still, the notebook would tell me that I hadn't made the whole thing up.

I paged through it one last time and came to a poem that we'd never worked into a song.

Death, like a flooding midnight stream,
sweeps us away, our life's a dream,

an empty tale, a morning flower,
cut down and withered in an hour.

Yeah, I could go back to Mount Hope and find all the graves again. Only it wouldn't be the same without Relly. We collected these olden-day words together. They weren't just mine. They were ours.

I held the notebook to my chest one last time, trying to squeeze the words into myself. Then I said goodbye and laid it on the fire.

The flames rose and ate the notebook. The wind swirled around, making a whirlpool. Heat, intense heat. Then the notebook was gone and cold returned. I was crying. I only noticed because the tears were freezing to my face.

When only ash was left, I went inside the house.

There was a message on the machine. While I was at the fire, Knacke had called. The little crimson dot pulsed like a bug full of blood. On, off, on, off.

I hit the play button.

"Come tonight," Knacke said. "You know where I live. And Relly will be set free."

OK, so I was going to Knacke's house that night. But what then? Would we all vanish in a puff of magic smoke, now that the tetrad was together again? Fly off to some other world where we'd rule as gods? Or would it be back to school again? A secret life there. Homework and assemblies one day. Hanging around with horrible old men the next.

I didn't now. And I guess I didn't really care. I was going to save Relly. That's all that mattered.

Two

IT SEEMED LIKE GODS SHOULD travel in style. A chariot, a glowing golden barge, maybe a flying carpet. Knacke should at least have sent a limo.

I went by bus. It was slow and I had to transfer downtown for the line that went out to the airport. I sat way in the back. Most of the trip I had my face pressed to the frosty window. Snow was coming in, wild gusts like flights of ghostly birds.

The lights of traffic, of the stores and houses we passed, seemed cold, like the rays of the moon, which give no heat.

We crossed the Broad Street bridge and I got a glimpse of the river, way below us. A stream of shiny blackness flowing due north. *Right here,* I thought. *This is the spot where Lissa had taken her life.* An old bum waved as we went past. I thought it was Scratch at first, standing guard. Only, he had to be at Knacke's place already.

My stop was the second from the end. Two old ladies were at the front of the bus. They were going to the airport, but not to travel. I figured they worked there as cleaners on the night shift.

The doors wheezed open and I climbed down. Going from the baked heat of the bus to the windy winter air, I felt a shock. All the way across the city, I'd been drifting in and out of a daze. Now I was wide awake, tongues of fear licking at my heart.

Everything except Knacke's house was closed up and dark. At his place, the windows were all bright and cheery, like this was Christmas Eve and he was expecting family any minute.

My finger stopped about an inch from the doorbell. I took a few deep breaths, getting myself ready for the fire dogs, for Knacke's bogus welcome. I closed my eyes and thought of Relly. I figured when this was all over, he'd understand why I came there. And maybe he'd want to thank me somehow.

Expecting an explosion of yapping and growling, I pressed the doorbell. Nothing happened. I did it again, leaning in close to listen. No cheesy chimes, no crazy barking.

Just for a minute, I thought I had the address mixed up. *Great, I come to the rescue and can't find the right house.*

I rapped my knuckles on the storm door.

A jet came pounding down out of the sky. The lights raked across Knacke's front yard. In the brilliant flash I saw a smoking black lump. Then the darkness rushed back.

Was it for real? Was it human? Now the fear was like a savage mouth that had swallowed my heart whole.

I went toward the burned heap in the lawn. I smelled something that made my stomach lurch upward. I managed to keep from throwing up, but just barely.

It was a dog in the front yard. And it had been burned like a huge overdone roast beef.

Suddenly, a car came ripping down the road. The headlights swept the yard and caught me like I was a prisoner trapped while making a jailbreak.

"Let's go!" a voice boomed. "Now! Get in the car." It was Frankengoon, loud as a police bullhorn. "Move!"

I did as I was told.

Frankengoon was behind the wheel. Scratch was in the back seat. "Your precious little friend has taken off. Mr. Knacke's gone after him."

Three

SO THERE I SAT IN the front seat, thinking about those Stranger Danger movies we had to watch in grade school. I remembered all sorts of stuff from them, warnings and rules. Don't accept rides. Don't take candy from strangers. But never once had we been told what to do when the assistant principal pulls up in some seedy neighborhood and tells you to get in. Or when your bio teacher turns out to be an evil firegod who's kidnapped your best friend.

The car stunk. I guess that was from Scratch, who had on his nastiest old bum coat. His teeth were brown, like he'd been eating dirt by the handful. He didn't say much besides hissing "Yes, yes," as Frankengoon told me what we were going to do.

"We'll find your friend." I'd never heard anyone make that word sound so horrible. "And we're going to make sure he never runs away again."

Tearing down the road, we went through some red

lights, and practically killed a lady as she crossed in front of us. I guess when gods are using their full powers, they can drive as fast as they want. No golden heavenly chariots. But no police waiting to give us a ticket, either.

We drove north on Plymouth Avenue, toward the glittering lights of downtown. The snow had let up, I guess. But the wind kept stirring it into whirlpools and sudden blinding blasts. The huge Kodak and Xerox buildings loomed ahead, with a few windows winking off and on, and the tops lost in the night sky.

"The bridge," Scratch said. "Yes, the bridge."

Frankengoon turned onto Broad Street and slowed down.

"There. Up ahead." Scratch was leaning over the front seat, peering through the windshield. I could smell him: B.O., unwashed clothes, ancient coffee breath. "There he is," he hissed.

Knacke stood in the middle of the bridge, his arms raised and his head thrown back. Snow moved like brilliant curtains around him. Globes of fire glowed in both hands.

At first I thought it was a freestanding shadow that faced Knacke. Every move he made, the shadow made too. Only as we got close did I see it was Relly.

Knacke waved his arms, flames pouring out his fingertips. Relly did the same. Knacke punched at his own chest. And I saw a heart made of red burning coals. Relly copied that move exactly. It was horrible to see, fires glowing inside his naked rib cage.

Frankengoon stopped his car and told me to get out.

"Good, good," Knacke said when he saw us. "All together again. Now we can finish this up. All's well that ends well." He hawked up a gob of blue fire.

Frankengoon took me by one arm and Scratch took me by the other. They dragged me forward and threw me at Knacke's feet.

Knacke made a broad gesture and a ring of flame licked around me, there on the sidewalk. It burned at my legs. I choked on the foul, oily fumes.

Only then did Relly break his mimic trance. With a sweeping motion of his arm, he seemed to gather up the flame, take it into himself. In a second it was gone. Only the faint wisps of smoke remained. And they were soon swept over the river gorge and were gone.

Knacke laughed, the way a grownup might laugh at a little kid's cute trick. "Didn't I tell you, Zee? He's nothing compared to me." A jet of flame roared out of Knacke's outstretched hands. He aimed over my head. This was all for show. He was still trying to convince me that I should join him and his tetrad.

"He's a pitiful little cigarette lighter. And I am the

sun!" As though he'd flicked a switch, his face lit up brilliant as a car's headlight. "He's a little crumb of rust and I am a globe of burning gold."

Now Scratch and Frankengoon had Relly by the arms, dragging him to the edge of the bridge.

"He has promise. I don't deny that. He has the power," Knacke said. "But I have a thousand times more. And when you've linked yourself to us, Zee, then we shall defeat death itself."

Relly seemed to give up. No more fire from him. No more resistance.

"Dearly beloved," Knacke said, like he was a preacher and this was some evil wedding. "We are gathered as gods to welcome our fourth. We have come here to complete our tetrad. We have our offering and we have our newest, truest, youngest power."

I was in a daze, I guess. I listened and I watched. But this was all so unreal. I think part of my brain just shut down. Knacke's plan was clear now. They were going to toss Relly into the gorge as a human sacrifice. Right here where the ghost of the canal crossed the shadowy river. One was gone and the other was in darkness, though I heard the rushing black water. Right here at this place of power in the middle of the city.

Here the four directions crossed. North and south— the river. East and west—the canal.

Here was the perfect place to sacrifice one young god and welcome another.

The snow blew above our heads, parting and closing like gauzy curtains. I looked across the river. And as the whiteouts faded for a moment, there was the statue in the sky. A Mercury made of copper. A heavy metal god floating in the blizzardy air.

Frankengoon and Scratch had Relly up on the stone ledge now, ready to push him into nowhere. The river surged on below, secret and inky black. The sound was beautiful and horrible too. So much power, an endless north-rushing flood.

"We offer up this boy. We offer up his fire as a sacrifice." Knacke was yelling now, though his voice was swallowed up quickly by the wind. "We offer him up to open the way for our fourth. As he is taken by the river, so shall our Zee be taken by us. Welcome, Zee." He reached for my hand.

Four

"YOU PROMISED," I WHISPERED. "You said if I joined you, then Relly would be safe. You promised."

He clapped his hands to shut me up. Sparks blew out from his fingertips. Again, I tried to argue. And he yelled me down, his awful growls turning to flame in midair.

Knacke made a claw of one hand and dragged it downward. He left four glowing marks that hung like luminous ribbons. He snarled and I thought he would turn into a beast right there. A mad dog with fiery breath.

"Now?" Frankengoon asked.

"Now?" Scratch repeated, pressing Relly backward over the abyss.

"Now," Knacke said.

The squeal of tires and the drumming of a powerful motor broke the ritual moment. There, coming at us down Broad Street was the Buttmobile, like a black hammer slamming through the white veils of snow.

Butt aimed his van straight at us, like he wanted to smash us all, throw us plummeting into the gorge.

Knacke screamed, Scratch howled, Frankengoon groaned the word No like a foghorn blast.

Butt pounded his brake pedal and threw open the side door. He leaned out, grabbed Relly, and yanked him into the van. I heard Jerod's voice too, yelling for me to follow.

I guess the fever came back to me in a burning wave. Because what I saw next seemed so unreal, and what I did was impossible. Fearless now, or maybe so crazy that fear didn't even count, I grabbed the four quivering ribbons of light out of the air and whipped them across Knacke's face. I felt pain, real and intense, going deep. But it was like my hand was not connected to my brain. It just grabbed. I lashed Knacke with those four burning whips and he fell back, snarling like a wild animal.

When my blurred daze fell away, I was in the Buttmobile, speeding with my three friends away from the bridge.

Relly was in bad shape, real bad shape. He'd looked at death and death had looked back at him. The abyss had been ready to take him. And he'd been ready to go. Now he was safe again, at least for a little while. Only it was like that black emptiness was still looming before him.

Butt had his foot to the floor. The van was shaking and tires whined as we took the snow-slicked corners. I was with Relly in the back, holding him, trying to get him all the way back to us. He shook. And this made me hold on tighter, like maybe I could draw some of the fear and the fire into myself.

"We're in big trouble!" Jerod yelled. "They're right behind us."

Relly's shakes started in again, worse than before. "There's no way," he whispered. "We're dead. We'll never get away from them."

Through the van's muddy rear window came two powerful streams of light. There was Knacke's car, with all three of our enemies in it. Their faces looked like white rubber masks, bulging and twisting in rage.

Five

"RELLY!" BUTT YELLED BACK. "Do something. Now! He's cooking the engine." Butt pointed to a dial on the dashboard. The little orange needle was tapping all the way to the right. "We'll burn up in about two minutes."

Relly crawled to the front. Already the smell of roasted rubber and scorched metal filled the van.

Wisps of poisonous green steam floated from under the dashboard.

"Do something!"

Relly tried to concentrate on the van's motor, drawing out the excess heat. He started to sweat and shake again. I put my arm around him, but drew back quickly. "Stop it! This isn't going to work. It'll kill you," I said. His fever cooked right through his coat. It hurt, bad. And it scared me. But I went back and hugged him again. Fever came out of him like venom from a snakebite. Out of him and into me.

Now smoke was billowing from under the hood. I

could hear the heat gauge ticking like a bomb. Relly let out a breath that stunk of car exhaust.

"We're dead," he said. "We'll never escape them."

A sudden bloom of red light filled the windshield.

"It's on fire!" Butt yelled and slammed on the brakes. "Out! Out! Get out now!"

He lunged from the driver's seat. I yanked crazily at the door handle. "Come on!" Butt was shouting. Flames shot from the van's front end. I stood there looking stupidly at the broken lever in my hand.

Relly finally came all the way out of his trance. He grabbed me by the arm and dragged me from the van.

We hadn't run far when the whole van was swept into a ball of flame. "Let's go!" Jerod yelled, shielding his eyes.

The van had come to rest right at the front gate of Mount Hope Cemetery. The hills, the bare trees, the endless ranks of white stones faded in and out of the snowstorm.

Mount Hope was locked up for the night. Relly, me, and Jerod were skinny enough to squeeze between the iron gates and flee inside. Butt, being a lot bigger, couldn't get through. He rattled the bars frantically, spitting curses.

Now Knacke's car had pulled up right behind the van. As the headlights died, the fire suddenly stopped, like it had been sucked into a gasping hole in the earth.

All three of us were yanking on the gate now from the inside. "Under. Under!" I yelled. Butt threw himself to the ground and crawled beneath the rusty bars. His coat caught and ripped. But he made it through.

We were in Mount Hope, and for a few minutes at least, the spiked iron fence would protect us from Knacke and the others.

"Come on!" I shouted, and we ran up the cobblestone roadway into the graveyard.

Six

WE REACHED THE TOP of the first hill. Below us, Knacke struggled to break through the gate. Flames seethed from his hands. Even from a distance, the groan of old melting iron was sickening.

In the olden days, Mount Hope was called the Beautiful City of the Dead. But that night, it seemed more like an entire country. There were hundreds of little hills, roadways that led everywhere and nowhere. Below, in the first valley, a few dozen tombs were laid out like an ancient stone village. In the other direction stood arches of stone, pyramids of stone, eight-sided shafts, and tiny stone churches.

"We can't win," Relly panted. "There's no point in running." No matter where we fled, our tracks would be perfectly clear to Knacke.

I paused a minute, turning inside myself. I was a god of water. Underground streams, yeah. The river, yeah. But also snow and ice. I let myself feel the water pouring through me. And I let myself feel the icy wind. Soon the snow was ten times thicker in the air. And our tracks were blotted out.

We ran on, into the hills where two hundred thousand people lay in eternal sleep.

I saw a tree stump full of water, like a rotted black cauldron. I saw a carved angel whose arms had fallen off and whose face had dissolved. Still, I could tell she was looking heavenward. I saw rank after rank of stones like soldiers hunched over in the drifting snow.

Knacke got through the gate and aimed his car up the first rattling brick roadway. I heard him somewhere behind us. Then I saw the bright jets of his headlights poking through the empty branches above us.

"We're dead, we're dead," Relly moaned. "We can't outrun a car."

"No, but we can hide far from the road."

He stopped, blowing on his fingers and stamping his feet. "We'll die of the cold or they'll get us. What difference does it make?"

"I don't get it," I said. "Why, after everything we went through, why are you giving up?"

"Because *you* did."

"What are you talking about?"

"You sold us out! You agreed to join up with Knacke."

"That was to save you!" I yelled. "I thought if I went with them—"

Relly tripped and went headlong into the snow. I grabbed for his hand, but he slapped it away. "You gave up on us," he hissed at me.

"I did not! I was trying to save your life."

We looked down at the marker that had caught his foot. It was a dissolving white lamb, a gravestone for a little child. "Just one year old," I said. "Didn't even have a name. 'Our Baby.' " For a hundred and fifty winters, the lamb had stood guard over this spot.

"We should just give up," Relly said. "I'm freezing to death. I can't keep going all night." He rolled onto the grave and rested his head on the lamb like it was a pillow.

I'd read somewhere about people freezing to death, how they get warm first and sleepy. "You got to keep moving," I said. "Come on. It's not much farther."

"What's not much farther? More graves, more snow?"

"Shhh!" Butt said.

The wind died suddenly, as though commanded to lie down. Footsteps were approaching. Three men, three old killer gods, coming at us from three directions.

Seven

WHITE SPECTERS LOOMED AROUND US. Winged angels, weeping angels, angels in triumph, and angels overwhelmed with sadness.

I peered into the snowy gloom and saw Frankengoon. He reached out, as though his arm might stretch over a hundred graves and grab me. I caught Jerod's eye. For a second, our minds locked and we pulled down more snow from the sky, a sudden howling blast. Then a force from the darkness fought back and made the winds quiet again.

"Jerod!" I shouted. I looked around frantically for him. But he'd fled, driven off by Frankengoon's far greater power. So it was just him against me, young water against ancient air. If anyone had been watching, all they would've seen was a kid cranked down inside herself and a huge hulking old man. He was grabbing at the sky like he could command the winds to do his will. I was hunched over, drawing up the water of the earth.

Up and down, it didn't make any difference now. A river seemed to flow in the sky. Snow and sleet seemed to rise from the ground. God or girl? Man or monster? Fever cooked my brain, set my blood simmering. Icy wind and burning breath—I couldn't tell the difference.

Knacke emerged from the blowing darkness. Both his hands were full of flame. And his eyes too, like two tiny suns. He yelled at us, only it wasn't words. The sound came out as a fiery viper's tongue. Snowflakes pelted the tongue, hissing into dots of steam.

I went toward Knacke, ready to fight even if it meant dying. "Zee!" Relly yelled. "Back off!" He was himself again, calling up a last flicker of inner flame to protect me.

Knacke met him, old fire struggling against new. The last battle of the burning gods. It was beautiful, like the dance of two creatures made of rushing flame. And at the same time, it was awful to see, each one fighting to draw the life, the light, the heart's fire, out of the other.

Where they fought, the snow ran away in dark streams.

"Water plus earth," I whispered. Then louder, to Butt. "Water plus earth equals mud." I grabbed him, yelling, "Do it. Now!"

He understood. We'd done it before. Now together we melted the side of the hill. I mean it got soft, oozy, unstable. A sick groaning came from below us, as though the hill itself was in pain. Trees started to tilt over. Gravestones tipped and slid. Great slabs and shoulders of mud began to collapse downward. Shouts and curses. Fire and smoke. Rivers of mud like the blood of the earth poured out. A huge grave marker leaned, then fell and took a few trees with it.

Now coffins were poking out of their holes. Dripping webs of tree roots grabbed at the empty air. A chunk of iron picket fence slid down the muddy hill like a sled with no rider.

Falling, I grabbed for Butt. Only he was already gone, pulled into the muck. Knacke and Relly, Scratch and Frankengoon, too. I was the last one standing.

Right below me, a coffin slid from its ancient hiding place. The lid caught on a huge root and was thrown aside. I saw a pale gray dress, like something woven out of spider thread. I saw a bony white face and long hair.

Then I lost my footing and was gone, like the others. Down, down, down.

Eight

THE FEVER SAVED ME, I guess. The poison heat I'd drawn out of Relly's body kept me alive while I lay there in the rising drift.

Snow was falling again. Not snow called by battling gods. But regular, real, normal snow.

I went in and out of feverish dreams. *I'm dead,* I thought. *This is what it means to be dead. Perfect silence. Cold and hot at the same time. Lost, alone, nowhere.*

Did I escape from that snowy grave like a ghost? I don't know. But I did rise and walk. I'm sure I left that place at the foot of the hill. Maybe my spirit came out from my body. Maybe some part of me split away. Or maybe the fever and the fight had made me completely crazy.

Whatever it was, however you explain it, I started moving in the snowstorm after my body came to rest.

A grave lay open. The coffin was empty.

I looked at myself and saw a long dress from the olden

237   Beautiful City of the Dead

days. Gray tatters. My hands were thin as bone. I took a deep breath and heard an empty rattle.

Before me was a stone that read SILENCE LOUD. Before me was her grave, a gaping hole.

Now deep in earth, this bed of sighs
I wait till I, like fire, shall rise.

The poem was true. She'd risen, and I'd risen, like fire. Not leaping flames, but a slow, powerful glow.

I was alive and I was her. I was me, Zee, the girl who never talked. And I was Silence too, awakened from her long sleep.

The air, swirling with snow, seemed to glow. All was peace and stillness. A beautiful silence had fallen on Mount Hope.

I was both dead and alive. Me, Zee, and she.

For a minute, or maybe an hour, I stood in the falling snow. Or maybe it was forever. Or only a second. I don't know now. It's all a brilliant blur, my memory cooked with fever and frozen by the winter air.

I stood there, we stood there. Surprised to rise. Me and she. The girl dead over a hundred years and the girl dead for five minutes.

There in the swirling snow was a black carriage and two black horses. People with black streamers on their hats and sleeves stood in a little circle. Mourners, I thought. They've come to see their Silence buried.

Mother and father, brothers and one sister. A preacher. Friends and distant relations. All there to see Silence Loud lowered into the grave.

"Wait," I said, but no one heard me. "Wait for me. I will be back someday."

Then something shifted. A deeper glow was burning in the blizzard. The people and the hearse flickered out of sight and I knew these were just Silence's last memories. Her spirit had hovered there in Mount Hope and seen her people lay her to rest.

The glow grew stronger, like a searchlight burning through heavy fog.

This brilliant fire was no memory. It was real. And it found me out.

"You," came Knacke's knife-edge whisper. He paused between every word. "You . . . will . . . pay . . . with . . . your . . . life."

That almost made me laugh. What was he going to do? Kill somebody who was already dead?

I went toward him. Silence and me, together, we went bravely to meet Knacke's last eruption of fire.

Straight at him. A rickety body that had been in the ground for almost two hundred years. We swayed and tottered. But we did not fear him anymore.

He was yelling now, I suppose. Curses and threats that had no power. He had gathered his flame for one final, awful blast. It came and it hurt worse than anything I'd ever felt. But it didn't stop us, me and Silence.

We grabbed him around the neck while the flames poured out. And we closed our bony feverish hands on his windpipe. Without oxygen there is no fire. We squeezed while he burned. And then the fire was gone. Gone for good.

Nine

THEY FOUND ME IN A snowdrift. That's what Relly said when I finally came back from nowhere.

I was in the hospital, and when the long fever-cold sleep finally ended, Relly was there.

For a long time, I kind of drifted in and out of the real world. Nurses were moving around, and my dad, too, I think. A doctor with a foreign accent came and looked in. And then a doctor with cold, soft hands. More nurses, messing with my IV drip. Butt and Jerod, maybe, and then a doctor who smelled of powerful soap.

When the death-haze lifted at last, Relly was there.

He looked pretty bad. Thinner and kind of washed out. Scratched and banged up from falling with the mudslide. The red-purple of his eyes made his skin look even paler. "You're going to be all right."

That was the first thing I remember him saying.

I guess the look I gave him said I didn't believe it.

Weakness filled me to the brim. I couldn't even move my head to one side.

"Really and truly," he said. "You're going to be all right."

Later, when I was a little more with it, he told me how they found Knacke burned up, dead and black like a stick pulled out of an old campfire. Frankengoon got swept into the mudslide. He survived, but he wasn't at school anymore. Scratch had just disappeared.

"Jerod's fine. I think he took off when things got too heavy. And Butt's OK," Relly said. "No major damage." Relly came closer and whispered, "You know: the god of dirt. He was in his element."

I wanted to ask a hundred questions. Only I had no voice. Nothing came out when I tried to talk.

The nurse returned and shooed Relly away. I fell back asleep. But it was normal sleep, not a fever haze with dead girls come alive and burning men dying.

Ten

I WAS IN THE HOSPITAL FOR A WEEK. Usually they treat
pneumonia with meds and let you go. Relly told me later I was
pretty near gone, fighting weaker and weaker to take a breath.
They had to run a tube into me, and that whole time is gone,
too. I guess they drugged me up pretty good beforehand.

When they finally let me go, I had no voice at all. The
nurse said that's normal for people who've been on the
breathing machine.

Yeah, normal. That made me feel just fine.

What was normal after you fought enemy gods to the
death? What did normal mean after you walked around a
graveyard inside the body of a girl buried two hundred
years ago?

"You'll be hoarse for a while. That's to be expected.
Soon enough you'll have your voice back." The nurse
gave me a big plastic smile and went back to filling out
the paperwork so I could leave.

A doctor came in to give the final OK. A few hours later my dad took me home.

Eleven

I WAS ALL SET UP IN my room to recover. Sound system within reach. A buzzer my dad rigged up to call him if I needed anything. All the junk food in the world.

Still, I had no voice. So my dad got a brand-new notebook for me, and a handful of pens.

The first night home, Silence was there with me. I don't mean some cheesy ghost went floating around the room. It was more like I'd brought her back from Mount Hope inside me. Thoughts drifted up, memories I was sure were hers. Names of people I'd never known. Old songs I guess she'd sung in church.

That was the weirdest part. I could hear melodies and words in my head. And I was positive they'd come from the olden days. They had the same stiff rhymes as the gravestone poems. In fact, I wrote this all out to Relly and he went looking in Mount Hope.

He came to visit the next day and said, "You were

right. I found one." He handed the page back to me.

> *Then let the last loud trumpet sound*
> *and bid our kindred rise;*
> *awake ye nations under ground;*
> *ye saints ascend the skies.*

I read the words, moving my lips but making no sound. I tried to say them. All that came out was a rattling hiss. I tried again. Nothing.

Still, in my head, the melody was going powerful and sure. I heard a voice, the voice of Silence Loud, singing this creaky song from the olden days. She had a beautiful voice. Sadness and gladness mixed together. Strength and weakness, too. I wanted so bad for Relly to hear it.

That's what I wrote to him on the notepad. "You should hear what it sounds like. It's great. Totally great. When I get my voice back, I'll show you."

Twelve

BUTT CAME FOR A VISIT, TOO. He gave me the latest news about school. "Knacke's dead. They're hushing the whole thing up. But everybody knows. And Frankengoon's gone, too. They're saying he's on a leave of absence. Only the rumor has it he's gone for good. We got this new guy. He always wears this hideous checkered coat and flood pants. I think his name is Bob Hein. Only everyone calls him 'Mr. Behind.' Get it? Get it?"

I got it.

"OK. So you get better real fast and we can start practicing again. All right?"

I nodded.

Relly got my Ibanez out of its case the next time he came. I hadn't touched it since the Bug Jar gig. That seemed like about a hundred years ago. "You should start playing a little," Relly said. "Keep the songs in your fingers, you know?"

I nodded and took the bass. It felt ten times heavier than I remembered. The strings were cold. Yet when I fit my hand around the neck, the old good feeling started to come back.

With no amp, you can hardly hear a bass. That was OK, at least at first. It was just for me. Nobody else had to hear the riffs that had been playing themselves in my inner ear. Soon enough, Relly would, and Butt and Jerod, too. First, though, I wanted to get them exactly right.

When I was alone I listened to Silence singing in my head. My fingers moved on the Ibanez, finding the sound, matching the melody.

Awake ye nations under ground;
ye saints ascend the skies.

I wondered how long Silence would be with me. She made it easier to sleep. I mean, her voice was kind of a night-light. It didn't shine. Nobody could see it. But it reassured me like the faint quavering bulb used to when I was little.

Thirteen

AFTER A WEEK, I WAS on my feet again. When I practiced, I pressed the headstock of my bass against the closet door and that made it a little louder. It got the wood vibrating. And I wondered if the whole house was sounding too. Real quiet, below hearing. But still shaking with the bass line throb.

Relly came over every day after school. We never talked about what happened in Mount Hope. No mention of gods and fire and tetrads. Maybe he thought it would set me back and I'd never get better again. Or start the fever burning again. Everyone was real upbeat, saying I'd be fine soon.

Still, my dad took me to an ear, nose, and throat specialist. "You're a lucky girl," he said after he heard about them finding me freezing in the snowdrift.

Yeah, real lucky, I thought.

He poked and prodded and stared into my mouth with bright lights. Then he ran some tests.

"There's been some bruising and minor abrasion," he said. "This is normal. Your vocal cords are medically healthy. I see no reason why your voice should not return fully to its normal functioning."

Right, normal. Everything was going to be normal.

Back at home it was just me and Silence, with our memories all tangled together. Singing in church—which I'd never done. Taking care of little brothers and sisters—which I never had. Working in the fields—which I had no idea how to do. These were the memories of her life. It was all so weird to me. But I guess it was normal for her.

So, I wondered, did she know about Ghost Metal now? And playing bass at the Bug Jar? Did she understand about Relly and the band?

It was almost funny, thinking about Silence in the pioneer days, with Black Sabbath and Judas Priest tunes running in her head while other people were singing holy hymns in church.

Fourteen

THAT NIGHT, I TOLD Silence I wanted my voice back.

She hadn't taken it. That's not what I mean. It was more like as long as she was inside me, I had to listen, not talk. *I want my voice back*. I thought those words, because I couldn't even manage a whisper.

Did she hear? I guess so. As long as she was inside me, our thoughts were like talking. Words would run in my head. And she'd reply with pictures and music and even smells from the olden days.

Her memories would open up and out would pour the smells. Wood smoke. Unwashed clothes. Bread rising. Bitter lye soap. Wildflowers. Mashed corn cooking in a big iron kettle.

The smells came with her voice. Maybe that's why it seemed so strange. You know how perfume kind of floats around somebody? Leaves a trail? That was what it felt like. I heard the melodies first, and then Silence thinking in my head. And then I smelled the olden days.

I'm afraid, real afraid. I want my voice back, I told her.

In reply came her lonely, sweet voice, singing to me from beyond the grave.

Blessed are those who silently wait
for they shall pass the beautiful gate.

I didn't tell my dad or the doctor or anyone else about the voices. They'd lock me up in a minute. Or pump me full of psych meds. It was bad enough being mute, let alone having them all think I was out of my mind too.

I didn't even tell Relly at first. No, I just figured out the songs and taught them to him on my bass. I had him go back to Mount Hope and find the gravestone poems that Silence had sung to me. A few were just fragments. Some were complete.

"We'll get them all down," I wrote in my notepad. "And then we'll record them all."

"That's right," he said. It was almost a whisper. "Ghost Metal."

Fifteen

THEN THE TIME CAME when I was better enough to play. I mean really play, back in Relly's attic, plugged in and turned up loud.

My dad drove me over to Slime Street. I went to the front door and Tannis was waiting, like the other times.

She let me in and we stood there in the kitchen not talking. Only we were OK now. I knew that without her saying a word. I'd done the right thing. She understood that. And a whole lot more now. She knew me for who I really was. And I was OK.

Then Relly came in and said, "All right! Time to kick out the jams. You ready?"

I nodded.

He'd run an extension cord up the stairs and had an electric heater cranking on high. So even though the snow was falling and the wind was moaning, we were nice and warm in the attic.

Butt gave me a huge welcome-back grin. And Jerod, too, was happy to see me on my feet again. "We missed you," he said. And I think he meant it.

"So what do you wanna play?" Relly asked.

I didn't need my little notepad for the answer. I just formed the words *Silence Loud,* and Relly got it. We had lyrics for the tune, the poem off her gravestone. Relly handed Jerod the lead sheet.

"Now deep in earth, this bed of sighs," Jerod said, getting the feel of the song.

Then Relly fired off the opening riff. Butt laid down the beat, old doom and new joy mixed together. "I wait till I, like fire, shall rise," Jerod sang. And then again, louder, wailing sure and true.

I was the last one to join in. I had a bass line all worked out, of course. I'd been waiting weeks for this moment. My fingers closed on the strings, pressed them hard to the frets. Butt and Relly were locked in, repeating the four-bar intro. Louder and louder, fierce as a war cry.

"OK," I whispered into the pounding noise.

I joined in, doubling Relly at first, then splitting off to coil our riffs together. It was great, it was huge, it was endless. The song rose, churning and sucking everything in like a cyclone.

"Then will my voice in great goodbyes," Jerod screamed from the speakers. "Join to the chorus of the skies."

Silence was inside me, riding the Ghost Metal tornado. Right at the center, at the heart of the song.

I didn't need a voice. I had the bass. I didn't need to hear myself talk or sing. Jerod could make the words for me.

Or maybe it was Silence herself, pouring out through the PA system. Either way, any way, they were my words. And all the world would hear them.

fire   *earth*   *wind*   *water*